When Mary Leary decides to leave home on June 1, 1981, at 3 P.M., it is no snap decision. She has been planning this ever since she heard Dr. Sally Page, an assistant professor of sociology at Georgetown University, give a speech on women's issues. Actually, it wasn't the speech itself that got Mary going, but the uncomfortable contrast she saw between Sally Page and her own "smothering" mother. Mother, staunch Catholic, homebody, and head of the Washington chapter of Life Chance, is part of Mary's Wonderful Family, which also includes her too glamorous sister Maud, her slightly spacey brother Eliot, and her absent-nearly-all-the-time father.

Mother tends to interfere in Mary's life because Mother is not entirely satisfied with Mary:

> Mary is too heavy.
> Mary doesn't do well in school.
> Mary has no Purpose in Life.
> Et cetera, et cetera.

Mary flees her mother and her Wonderful Family to live with Dr. Sally Page and *her* family, at least for the summer. But life on the other side of the fence has its complications as well: Sally's husband, the ex-Reverend Page, leads a Death Group; little blond Albert Page bites; and Sally's strange but attractive brother Zeke wears dresses and wigs. All of them take Mary in and take her by surprise.

The Revolution of Mary Leary

SUSAN SHREVE

ALFRED A. KNOPF NEW YORK

*Manufactured in the United States of America
1   2   3   4   5   6   7   8   9   10*

*Library of Congress Cataloging in Publication Data
Shreve, Susan Richards.
The revolution of Mary Leary.
Summary: During the summer before her
senior year, a Catholic girl runs away from
her well-meaning but narrow-minded mother
and finds a job as a mother's helper.
[1. Runaways—Fiction.   2. Mothers and daughters
—Fiction.   3. Babysitters—Fiction]   I. Title.
PZ7.S55915Re   1982   [Fic]   82–185
AACR2
ISBN 0–394–84776–8
ISBN 0–394–94776–2 (lib. bdg.)*

for CONNIE CALLAHAN RICHARDS
with love and admiration

The Revolution of
Mary Leary

1

The Declaration of Independence

I decided to leave home on a beautiful Monday afternoon the first of June, around three o'clock. It will sound like a snap decision when I tell you the circumstances, but it was not. In fact, I've been coming to this decision for the same number of years I've been a conscious member of this Wonderful Family. This is the way my mother describes us with her predictable enthusiasm for the wrong things, as you will see.

This afternoon I went out to the backyard to study for my U.S. History examination at the National Cathedral School, where I'm a junior. It was quarter to three, and my mother was on the telephone with Aunt Ethel, talking about the Life Chance March she's leading to the Capitol on June twentieth. Life Chance, I should hasten to tell you, is a national Catholic organization founded by Mrs. Michael O'Ryan, mother of eleven from Minneapolis, whose sole purpose is to prevent the use of contraceptives. Honest to God. So I thought I could study U.S. history in peace for a couple of hours—the general length of my mother's conversations with Aunt Ethel—and not have a Serious Discussion with Mother about my academic problems, which is why I have academic problems in the first place, because the time I should be studying is taken by Serious Discussions with Mother.

I like our backyard. It is small, like most backyards in Georgetown, but full of flowers, and I like working here more than anyplace I know as long as I turn my back on the statue of St. Michael that Mother purchased at auction when St. Cecilia's went to high rises (which should have been a Sign to her) and gave to my father for his fiftieth birthday, unaware that he only believes in God to keep their marriage in order. He hates the statue of St. Michael, which is pure white and stands six feet tall. Any self-respecting man would object to St. Michael filling his garden.

I was mistaken about Mother and Aunt Ethel because I had only opened to the first chapter of U.S. history when she came down the back steps with a bowl of chocolate chip cookies and lemonade. She was, I could tell, ready to settle in for a Serious Discussion.

My mother is a large woman—"handsome" my father says, but of course, he has his prejudices; "fat" my younger brother says, which is more to the point—and I look like her except I have glasses. Neither of us should be eating a bowl of chocolate chip cookies, which I point out to her too late, after we have both eaten half a dozen, maybe more.

"You have to like yourself," Mother says to me, "and you can't like yourself if you weigh too much."

I don't disagree, but it is difficult to go on a diet in this family because Mother believes Conversation, which is how she describes her lectures, sufficient solution, and she cooks endlessly.

"Why did you bring the cookies, then?" I ask.

"If you're trying to lose weight, don't eat them," she says to me.

"If you want me to lose weight, don't bring them," I say to her. We have a great deal of conversation about food in this Wonderful Family.

"I'm trying to study history," I say to my mother.

"That's just what I came out to talk to you about," Mother says. "I talked to Mr. Owens." Mr. Owens is my U.S. History teacher and he is among the several teachers at National Cathedral whom my mother advises on book lists, a situation which is tolerated only because my father is, as my mother says, a Very Important professor at Georgetown Law School, and on the board at Cathedral.

"I know," I say. "Mr. Owens told me."

"He says you're Very Smart, Mary, Very Smart."
My mother speaks in upper- and lowercase letters.

"I know," I say.

For years Mother has been telling me in our
Serious Discussions that I'm Very Smart or else that
one of my teachers has told her I'm Very Smart and
not living up to my high potential and so on and so
forth. I can only imagine how depressed I'd be if I
were living up to my potential.

"He says that if you read the history"—she
pauses, all uppercase—"READ, you would do
brilliantly."

"That's exactly what I had in mind doing this
afternoon, Mother. Until you came out, I was
planning to READ my history."

"Good," she says. And then she brings up Eliot.
I can count on the fact that Eliot will be brought up
in any Serious Discussion about my shortcomings.
He will be mentioned as a member of our Wonderful Family who either doesn't have shortcomings or
else has overcome them—the latter, of course,
preferable to my mother who, in keeping with
Judgment Day Christianity, likes to see victory in
overtime.

My brother, Eliot, is sixteen and thin. He is not
very smart, my mother likes to point out to
me—and, I assume, to Eliot—but he works hard
and does well. I happen to know that whatever
the limitations of Eliot's intelligence, he is smart
enough to "shut up," a suggestion he commonly

makes to me. I happen to know that he doesn't work hard, if at all, but he has discovered that the fundamental secret to our institutional world is anonymity and has become a master at it. I also happen to know that wonderful hardworking Eliot is at this very moment, seconds before my final decision to leave home for good, in the basement of my mother's house, smoking dope as he does every afternoon with his friend Pauline, and watching the soaps.

"I don't particularly want to talk about Eliot," I tell my mother. "I'd prefer reading U.S. history." For emphasis I get up, go in the house, answer the telephone, which is ringing, and tell Aunt Ethel, who is at the other end of the wire, that Mother will be right there.

Eliot and Pauline are lying on the couch at opposite ends so that Pauline's feet are next to Eliot's head and vice versa, a fact I point out to illustrate their states of mind. In order for me to lie willingly next to Eliot's feet, I'd have to be unconscious. They are staring at the ceiling, which is white soundproof board, broken in places where Eliot threw his baseball when he was a major league baseball player, before this particular phase of adolescent retirement began. I cannot imagine what interest the ceiling holds for Eliot and Pauline, but then I can't imagine what interest they hold for each other either.

"I'm leaving home," I say to Eliot.

"Honest?" Pauline says. "When?"

I'm not going to say very much about Pauline because I imagine this phase in Eliot will be short-term, followed by a worse one that will not include Pauline, but primarily I'm not going to say anything because there isn't much to say about her. She bubbles. When she isn't smoking dope with Eliot, she bubbles ferociously.

"No substance," my father says of Pauline, but I should add that my father finds no substance in anyone but my mother, and, I would expect, his accountant.

"Today," I say. So far Eliot has not responded to this information. Now he opens his eyes and stretches his legs next to Pauline's head.

"Where are you going?" he asks.

"I know where I'm going," I say, which I do, of course, but that will come later. "I'm not going to say where I am until I get settled," I say. "I'm smothering in this Wonderful Family."

"Listen, Mary," Eliot says. He always says *listen*, as though it will be worthwhile listening, and—good Catholic girl that I am—I always listen. "You and Mom will work this problem out."

"You don't work out smothering," I say.

He pulls himself up on the couch.

"Are you honest-to-God leaving?"

"I'm honest-to-God leaving."

"Jesus Christ," Eliot says mildly. "It's no big deal

around here, y'know. Look at me. Mother leaves me alone. She hasn't been down once. Right, Pauline?"

"Right," Pauline says with her usual candor.

"You only have to finish one more year in school, and then you can get married or go to Europe or something. You know, anything you want. It'll be swell."

That is Eliot's idea of adulthood. Anything you want. The terrible thing about it is that Eliot will probably have that kind of adulthood. Eliot has had anything he wants in childhood, and there's no reason for him to expect a change. If he has an internal life with dimensions beyond the ones visible to me right now as I watch him lying next to Pauline with his red eyes half closed, that life is a well-kept secret. I like Eliot. I like him in spite of myself.

"You're just not laid-back enough, Mary," he says to me. "This will pass." Honest to God. And he's *perfectly* intelligent even though he's stoned three quarters of the time.

"So will my life pass," I say to him overdramatically, but that's one of my shortcomings. I don't, however, want you to think that my evaluation of this family is overdramatic, or my decision to leave home. That is a calculated decision that began in earnest when my sister, eleven months older than I am, turned thirteen.

"See you around," Eliot says, and Pauline tries

to say something bubbly and sincere, but Eliot silences her with one blue-jeaned leg over her thigh.

"Let her go," he says, as though there is a thing he can do about it.

Mother is still talking enthusiastically to Aunt Ethel on the telephone. Mother is always enthusiastic, which is part of the trouble. She should have been either a nun and spent that energy on God, which would have helped his case, I can assure you, or the mother of fourteen children, so that her enthusiasm, particularly that expended against our sins, could have been divided in very small portions. As it is, my mother's Sole Purpose in Life is to be a Good Mother and raise the Wonderful Family she has raised. Except me.

> Mary is too heavy.
> Mary doesn't do well in school.
> Mary has peculiar friends.
> Mary has no Purpose in Life.
> Mary doesn't go to church even at Easter.
> Mary spends too much time in her room.

This is my mother's conversation with my father when he comes home in his usual bad mood from the law office where he works or the law school where he teaches, working as many hours as he possibly can, which does reflect on the pleasure he finds in our Wonderful Family.

Mary this
Mary that
Mary had a yellow cat.
Set him on the mantelpiece
Fifty pounds of candlegrease.

That's my state of mind.

"Don't mention Mary to me," my father says. I am not the bane of my father's existence. In fact, in a consideration of lesser evils, I am probably his favorite child because I remind him of my mother, which is the primary reason for my leaving—to avoid any further imitative tendencies on my part. If I turn out at forty-five to be like my mother, I will serve myself strychnine on chocolate marshmallow ice cream and die.

My father, understandably, does not like my sister, Maud, who calls herself Maud Gonne, after Yeats's lover, which tells you about as much as you need to know about Maud. And he is bored by Eliot, who, he says, "doesn't use the fine mind he was born with." My father is keen on using everything you were born with or acquire.

I pass my mother in the kitchen on my way upstairs to pack.

"I'll be right off," she calls to me as I pass. "I haven't finished talking to you yet."

"I know that," I say, but I'm also sure I have time to shower and pack and leave unobserved before Mother finishes with Aunt Ethel.

I pack my backpack and wear jeans. I take two skirts, three shirts, another pair of jeans, a sweater, a stuffed raccoon from a boy who kissed me when I was fifteen—even though, as he told me, he loved Sandy Layton—face stuff, plenty of shampoo, My Sin perfume, a bathing suit that I've had for only a month but which holds my form when I'm out of it as though in affection, and some good books I want to read. These are books that my mother would call "nihilistic," like *Lord of the Flies,* or "morally depraved," like *Women in Love,* or "terrible terrible terrible," like *The World According to Garp,* which I bought in hardback and have read twice already and almost kissed the face off John Irving's picture on the back.

At the last minute I go into Maud's drawer and take all of her bikini underwear: black lace, violet with ribbon borders, mauve, burgundy with beige lace—all but the flowered pair that I know for a fact she never wears since I see her every day in her underwear in her pantied parade by all the mirrors on the third floor, checking, I'm sure, although I've never mentioned it to Maud—we're not on those terms—her sweet, supple body with the eyes of Jonathan Nims, who screws her every weekend he's home from college in his parents' recreation room. This I know for a fact.

My mother thinks Maud is a wonderful girl, as you can imagine. "Pretty as a picture," my mother says, though our tastes in art have never been similar. She was first in her class in high school, vice president of the senior class, in the glee club and French club, and she's been on the Dean's List three straight semesters since she went to college. She goes out with Jonathan Nims, whose father is the senator from North Dakota (there couldn't have been much competition for his job in North Dakota), sews her own clothes, cooks dinner two nights a week, and, wonder of wonders, prefers sullen silence to talking back, the latter of which is my normal mode of expression. I don't need to tell you the effect of Maud's sullen silence on me. I have thought, not infrequently, of shutting her in the attic closet, where my father suspects, with good reason, that we have rats. Maud doesn't bring out the best in me.

My mother often talks to me about saving my body for the man I marry, as if at the moment I have any choice, but she guesses that given the choice, I'd never opt for waiting. I doubt she's ever had the body-saving conversation with Maud Gonne, believing, honest to God, that Maud is a virgin. Maud hasn't been a virgin since she was fifteen. I'd never say this to her, but I imagine that in a pinch she could sleep with a horse.

I take her new Golden-as-the-Sun lipstick and write on the mirror that she examines every minute she's home:

SEE YOU SOMETIME.
SISTER MARY.

I draw a picture of a fat girl in a nun's habit, which leaves only a quarter of a tube of Golden-as-the-Sun.

Mother is telling Aunt Ethel about Maud's plans for the summer. Maud is going to France to study French at the Sorbonne or boys in the Tuileries and then for the winter, when she transfers to the University of Pennsylvania, Maud plans to study art history because of her very great interest in art history. And that is the last I hear from Mother about the exemplary daughter in our Wonderful Family before I walk out the front door of our Georgetown row house in the bright June sunlight, leaving 2417 R Street, N.W., forever, Amen.

2
Early
Difficulties

I have not even gone down the first set of steps before Maud Gonne arrives in Jonathan's 1958 canary-yellow MG with the top down.

I do not have time to jump behind the rhododendrons—but, as you can imagine, I am not ecstatic to see the loving couple leap out of the MG without opening the doors.

"Boy, am I glad to see you," Maud says with more enthusiasm than seems necessary. I do not return the greeting. I am primarily concerned that she can see through my backpack with the X-ray eyes she has inherited from my mother's side of the family to her bikini underwear that I have stolen.

"I have a real problem," Maud says in a voice reserved for secrets. Of all times in my life that I am not interested in Maud's secrets, this moment is one of them.

"I'm kind of in a hurry," I say in my coolest voice.

"It'll only take a minute," she says. *I need money.* She mouths it, so Jonathan can't hear.

Maud has never in her life asked me for money before. I'm in a better position than I have ever been with her—and, as luck would have it, she catches me right in the middle of running away from home so I can't take advantage of this unusual situation.

Money I have. In fact, I have two thousand eight hundred and sixty-four dollars and twenty-eight cents saved from a lifetime of birthday and Christmas presents, baby-sitting for the Piagets next door and the Andromedas on Q Street, and money I've gotten from presents returned that didn't fit. I simply don't spend except in an emergency. And just at this very moment I am on my way to the bank to withdraw two hundred and fifty dollars in order to get traveler's checks in case of such an emergency.

I don't spend money except on a few things. I buy perfume, as you know, because I read somewhere that perfume is a real turn-on, and I need all the help I can get. I buy books, since the general reading material available in our house includes legal volumes, the complete works of St. Augustine, the writings of St. Francis of Assisi, several collections of Jesuit essays—I could go on, but you get the picture. So if I want to read something noncelibate, which is *all* I want to read, I have to buy it myself and hide it underneath my bed. I also buy Sea Breeze, and cotton balls in quantity, since my mother won't buy anything artificial, believing hot soap and water twice a day will clear up any adolescent problems. And she is, of course, dead wrong.

Maud, on the other hand, never has any money because she spends it on sweaters and knickers (she has five pairs, one velvet); clogs in suede and leather; cotton T-shirts that show her nipples; lip gloss, mascara, and blue eye shadow; and occasionally *Vogue* magazine, where she looks for new hairstyles. I could go on, but the subject is boring.

"I need *a lot,*" she says to me.

Jonathan has lit a cigarette and is leaning against the MG—sitting, in fact, on the hood. He has memorized magazines in which blond men in blue jeans smoke Pall Malls, leaning against their sports cars covered with girls. I am certain he couldn't hear us if we were screaming, because he is thinking about how wonderful he looks, et cetera et cetera.

"How much?" I ask Maud, mildly interested in this development in spite of my pressing plans to run away.

"Two hundred," Maud says.

"Jeez," I say, impressed. "That *is* a lot."

"I told you so."

I look at Maud, which is unusual, since I find it much better for my frail ego not to look at Maud, but today I notice that she looks *very* pale, that her delphinium-blue eyes are red around the rims, and that she hasn't blown-dry her hair, so it's lying flat as a towel around her head.

"What do you need two hundred dollars for?" I ask.

I never for a moment suspect that she will tell me. And she doesn't. But I have already guessed.

"I'll tell you later," she says.

It is her suggestion that I hop in the MG with Jonathan and we drive to the bank so I can withdraw the money and then they'll take me anyplace I want to go. But I better not say a word about the money to Jonathan. I am not interested in a conversation with Jonathan about anything, so I'm perfectly agreeable.

My idea of heaven does not happen to include riding on Maud's lap in the bucket seat of a canary-yellow MG down Wisconsin Avenue to M Street, where the National Bank of Washington is located. I don't particularly like Maud, but I don't want to be held responsible for breaking her legs because I was sitting on them either.

On the drive down Wisconsin Avenue I have plenty of time to make an alternative plan. Which is that I will get the money for Maud; wish her good luck, since my present intuition tells me she's going to need it; wave good-bye to the beautiful Jonathan Nims; and pretend to go to the Book Annex across the street. When they are well out of sight, I'll go back to the bank and get two hundred and fifty dollars in traveler's checks for myself.

It is disgusting how nice people can be to you when they want something.

"This is really terrific of you, Mary," Maud says while we're waiting in line for the teller.

"I'll pay you back as soon as I can," she adds without confidence.

"You are so smart to save your money," she says to me. "I wish I could learn to be better at that."

She is beginning to make me sick.

"Forget it," I say.

I hand her the two hundred dollars in a white envelope.

"Can we take you anyplace?" she asks me in a sweet voice.

"Nope," I say. "I'm going to the bookstore."

"Okay. I'll see you at dinner," she says.

It seems unnecessary to say that I won't be at dinner.

I watch the MG pull around the corner of M Street and disappear on its way, I suppose, to Georgetown University Hospital. It is astonishing to me that it's possible to have an abortion between three o'clock in the afternoon and dinnertime. But that is exactly what I imagine Maud Gonne is off to do with the two hundred dollars from my bank account.

Why else would she need two hundred dollars from me on the double? This is going to be a red-letter day for the mother of our Wonderful Family. But I don't have time for any Advance Sympathy.

I go back to the bank, take out two hundred and fifty dollars and buy my traveler's checks, and catch the Friendship Heights bus uptown to Newark Street.

3
The Other Side of the Fence

I am going to the Pages. That much I know. I know that the Pages live in Cleveland Park, which is an old neighborhood of Victorian houses about a mile from mine. I know that they have three children, at least a dog, probably a number of cats; that Mr. Page is the Reverend Page, presently—maybe permanently—unemployed because he ordained a woman in the Episcopal Church some time ago; and that Mrs. Page is Dr. Page, and she is an assistant professor of sociology at Georgetown University. I instinctively expect a great many other people live in their house in Cleveland Park, like the woman, also unemployed, whom the Reverend Page ordained against orders, and I can imagine that people are invited as studies for Dr. Page's sociological papers and simply don't leave. That is precisely why I am going to the Pages. The only real problem with this arrangement is that the Pages are not expecting me.

My intuition tells me that I will go up to their front door at 3411 Newark Street, Dr. Page will answer—carrying a baby in one arm and holding the collar of a barking dog with the other—and I'll say: "Hello. I'm Mary Leary, and I've left home and come to spend the summer with you."

Dr. Page will register no surprise whatsoever. She will step back to let me in, hand me what's-her-name, tell me the twins' supper is on the counter in the kitchen (and to stand back because they spit their vegetables), and that my room will be the yellow one at the right on the third floor. She is in a rush, and we will talk later. Which is, honest to God, how it happens.

I am not without good sense, and more than intuition leads me to the Pages when I leave home on the first of June. This will require some explanation because Dr. Page, whom I call Sally, had never met me formally until this afternoon.

I had seen her when she spoke to a group of freshman and sophomore women on Woman's Issues at Georgetown University in early May. I had reason to believe she would be glad to see me at her front door on Newark Street and equal reason to believe that my mother would prefer I moved in with the devil-in-drag than Dr. Sally Page of Georgetown University, as you will see.

Although Georgetown University, where Maud goes—and I will, in time—is a Catholic school, I didn't go to a Catholic high school. I used to, of course. We all did. But I smoked cigarettes in the ninth grade and was expelled for that and a bad attitude. It was terrible, and by the time I was in ninth grade, I would have done anything, no matter how dangerous, to be expelled so my mother should have been, and, of course, wasn't, grateful that I only smoked cigarettes. I wanted to go to public school and lose my virginity, which is what I thought happened to everyone in the first weeks of public school.

But Maud Gonne, Wonder of Wonders, was already at National Cathedral School, a fine upright place without boys or other diversions of any worth, and my father was on the board—he is on many boards, as a defense against free time—and my mother was a self-appointed morals committee at the school, so I went to National Cathedral, trailing on the slender ankles of the lovely Maud Leary, who was then a sophomore with a reputation for perfection.

In the first weeks I was there, I said I was adopted. There have been a number of occasions in my life when I've said I was adopted, but unfortunately even the calves of my legs are like my mother's.

There is not much to say about my association with National Cathedral. As you might imagine, I am not a star pupil or star athlete or star beauty or star cooperator or any of the other things generally revered at places like schools and exemplified by the wonder of wonders who sleeps in the bedroom next to mine, dreaming of Jonathan Nims. I keep a low profile. I don't smoke cigarettes. I didn't even like them when I smoked them at Our Lady of Ladies. I haven't been seriously kissed except by safe boys like the one I mentioned, who promised me it was a gesture of friendship. I get average grades, have a few friends, some of whom I like very much, but I keep my personal life to myself. Occasionally I explain that I was adopted and coincidentally look like my mother—adoption agencies are always trying to match people exactly.

Maud graduated from National Cathedral first and went to Georgetown because it was free, since my father teaches there, with the promise from my parents that she could transfer after two years, which is what she is doing. I will go there after my senior year because it will be the only place where I am accepted, also because of my father's teaching, so Maud and I will be back at the same school with no visible difference from National Cathedral, including my father's presence, my mother's presence, and the presence of God.

The afternoon that I saw Sally Page, I wished I had been adopted. I don't know what kind of stuffing Maud Gonne has in her brain that she can withstand the mother of our Wonderful Family when Mother gets going as she did with Sally Page this May, because, to survive afternoons like that one, I'd arrange for the same stuffing and forget my desire for slender ankles.

I should have known that Mother would be there in her loafers and pale pink tweed suit, sitting at the back of the auditorium so that when she spoke—and no one could possibly assume that she wasn't going to speak—everybody in the whole assembly could hear her.

Sally Page was billed as "a sociologist invited to speak on Women's Issues," particularly abortion. I should have known then. I should have come down with the flu that morning.

"Your mother is a tiger about abortion," my father says, which is about as poetic as my father gets.

"*Life,*" my mother says. She won't even use the word *abortion* publicly—fearful, perhaps, that the place reserved for her in heaven will be taken by Aunt Ethel. "I'm ferocious about life," she says.

We avoid the subject at home. It is worth hours. Mother has followed me into closets, into the bathroom, down R Street, once she's gotten started. She hands out pamphlets to the family. I'm not kidding. She can stand in my doorway after I've turned out my lights, turned on my radio, and closed my eyes, and talk about abortion as though

I'm a serious candidate. Maud Gonne misses a lot of these instructive lectures by being in the recreation room at Senator Nims's house.

Anyway there she was in the back of the auditorium at Georgetown University. She even had on red lipstick. No one could have mistaken the fact that she had been a bobby-soxer of the fifties, now a married mother with Social Concerns. I felt sick, but I have lived with my mother for a long time. It would not surprise me greatly if she arrived at my wedding bed with extra information and instructions for the next act. I have learned not to make a scene in public or cry or make faces or even recognize that the woman in the back of the room is related to me.

I wonder if I should tell Dr. Sally Page that I'm adopted, so she won't hold my genes accountable when Mother starts to organize the trouble that I know she is burning to organize. She has mentioned it twice on the telephone to Aunt Ethel and once to the priest while I was in the kitchen, and that was before I left home.

"Ethel," I overheard her saying while I was making a chocolate malt just recently. "There is a woman, a laywoman, not even a Catholic, teaching freshmen at Georgetown. And she's in favor of abortion."

I listened to hear whether Aunt Ethel had died on the spot.

"I have spoken to Father Harkness," Mother went on ominously.

I could imagine my mother in her blue shirt-waist dress, without makeup, sitting across from Father Harkness in the old walnut office in the tower of Georgetown University filled with pictures of Jesus in many poses and upholstered leather chairs.

"Father," my mother would say to the priest in a voice that sounds as if it had sustained years of injury. "I have come to you about Doctor Sally Page."

Dr. Sally Page is the kind of woman you'd like to have for a mother, especially if you're developing, as I am, fears about turning out like her. She is thin, for one, with straight hair, shoulder-length, that she doesn't curl. She doesn't wear lipstick. The day I saw her, she had on black trousers, a turtle-neck, and clogs. According to my mother, only men should wear trousers, but she hasn't been particu-larly effective in that campaign.

The speech Dr. Page gave turned out to be, just as I had feared, on abortion. It was about the history of women and their right to an indepen-dent choice. She was not suggesting that we all try out abortion for experimental purposes. She wasn't even recommending it, just presenting it as an alternative, which I told my mother, and you'd have thought I was considering living in an apartment in Jerusalem with King Herod. She even held me responsible for the stomach flu she came down with after Sally Page's speech. At least partially. The rest of the virus was sent to attack her by Sally Page.

Later, by a foolish mistake, I asked Mother why she had sent me to National Cathedral if it wasn't to learn to make intelligent and educated choices.

One thing I have noticed about Wonder of Wonders is that long ago, even before her first Communion, she learned the value of agreeable silence. I expect that she and Jonathan Nims could be pelvis to pelvis on the living room couch, and Mother wouldn't notice at all, as long as Maud sustained an agreeable silence.

There were a lot of questions after Dr. Page's talk, most of which didn't get answered because Mother stood up in the back of the auditorium in her tweed suit and round-collared blouse with a few questions of her own. Just as another sociology teacher, a soft potato-cake of a man, no match for Mother, stood up to suggest that some of the students might like to ask a question or two—not an astonishing observation on his part—Mother exploded.

"I am *deeply* concerned to hear you talk to these young women, Doctor Page," my mother said, expanding like a ruffled hen, filling the room with her presence. "These are women who look to you for an example of how to live life, and you are presenting them with methods for doing away with life."

"Not at all," Dr. Page began. But in the next ten seconds she learned not to interrupt.

"I have two daughters in this audience," my mother said. I opened a book of poetry and pretended to be reading.

And then my mother began her Life Chance platform, her voice rising as I would imagine the voice of St. Peter as though she were running in the primaries for the office of the Virgin Mary.

Once I looked at Maud Gonne, who was sitting in the front row with her splendid legs crossed, examining the length and shape of her fingernails. I considered interrupting my mother by shouting, "PERHAPS MAUD LEARY COULD SHARE WITH US SOME OF HER CONTRACEPTIVE PREFERENCES," but, as you can imagine, I thought better of it. In that brief time Before Mother, as in B.C., I noticed two astonishing things about Sally Page. One is that she is funny.

"Your mother is the funniest woman I know." Honest to God, my father says that all the time. "That's why I married her," he says, and I'm glad he can find a reason that is specific, but you will be relieved to know, after such hyperbole, that the only other woman my father knows is his secretary, Miss Parsons, and for humor, given the choice of Mother and Miss Parsons, Mother has a slight edge.

The second thing I notice about Sally Page is

that she listens. My mother was born with a congenital hearing problem, passed to her from my grandmother and now on to Wonder of Wonders, which allows Mother to hear only her own voice.

Sally Page even listened to Mother.

Fortunately Mother left immediately after giving her lecture. She prefers to make a hasty exit after her deliveries in the manner she must have learned from her Bible memorization of God's quick retreats following pronouncements. This, in any case, left me free to go up to Dr. Sally Page after her talk. I waited to be certain that Maud Gonne was not coming, was going instead to the ladies' room across the hall to reapply blush-on before going to Classics, which is taught by Father Ryan, who, I do not need to tell you, is a priest, a presumed celibate.

I didn't mention to Dr. Page that the woman at the talk was my mother. There is a degree of excess at which it is no longer possible to apologize for someone related, and my mother had reached that degree before I was born.

When I joined the group around Dr. Page, she was not talking about abortion but was asking if anyone would be interested in spending the summer at her house in Cleveland Park and helping her take care of twins, who were babies, and Albert, who was six. Even as she described the house and the animals (I don't even like animals), the visitors and guests who came, I could imagine myself, summer evenings, lying on a hammock on the front porch, talking about abortion with Dr. Page and about God with the unemployed Reverend Page, and certainly in a household of that size and energy, there would be someone between the ages of eighteen and thirty who would want to kiss me in more than a gesture of friendship.

I didn't mention a word of this to Dr. Page or that I was interested in spending the summer there, though several girls did, but I cataloged it away in my mind as I do most information that may, at one time, prove useful. For the next weeks I closed my eyes, imagining summer at the Pages', where, for the first time, I would be able to avoid Wonder of Wonders examining the angle of her hipbones in the mirror on the back of my bedroom door.

Which explains how I happen to arrive at the Reverend and Dr. Page's to take Cassie from Dr. Page into the kitchen, where I feed her dinner, and then into the living room, where a thin and rather beautiful man, around the age of Dr. Page—and so, I assume rightly, that it must be the unemployed Reverend Billy Page—is lying in a wooden casket.

He is not dead, although his arms are crossed over his chest in the usual manner of a corpse in a coffin. In fact, as I walk into the living room with Cassie he extends one of them to me, saying that he is Billy Page and asking if I am the baby-sitter for the night or will I be here longer. Sally had been in a rush and hadn't said. I tell him "longer," I do not say "forever," and he gets out of the casket and shows me where I'll be sleeping; where Cassie's twin, Thomas, is already asleep; where Albert would sleep were he not at his grandmother's, "Thank God"; and where I'll be sleeping.

When I come downstairs to report that Cassie is at last in bed, an hour and forty-five minutes later, which is the time it has taken me to get her there, the living room is full of people, several of whom must have brought their own caskets and are lying in them.

I go into the kitchen and clean the baby spinach off the floor where Cassie has thrown it at me.

A young man comes into the kitchen, opens the refrigerator, and takes out the orange juice, which he drinks from the pitcher.

"Are you in the Death Group?" he asks me.

"In the what?" I say.

"I guess you're not," he says. "You must live here."

"I think," I say, but I will not commit myself. Already I have a sense that life as a runaway might be more than I bargained for. And any moment now I expect to learn that Mother is making remarkable arrangements, from the telephone in the kitchen, that she hopes will determine my life in this house.

4

The Plight of a Dutiful Daughter

The cover story in *Redbook* magazine, which is lying next to the sugar bowl on the kitchen table, smudged with dry dough, is about abortion. I sit down on the stool and read the whole thing, interrupted only occasionally by a member of the Death Group coming in to check the refrigerator. The story is about a young woman named Jennifer —twenty-three, college-educated, unmarried, with a promising career in television—and her heart-rending decision to have an abortion. The man, who also has a promising career, sounds terrific to me and he even wants to marry her, which is her first mistake. She isn't ready—so much of her life ahead of her, et cetera, et cetera. Thus, the abortion. The story is told in explicit but understated detail, complete with the vacuum cleaner and the terrible guilt—a condition I know as well as the Lord's Prayer without near the provocation Jennifer has—and I'm sure the story was printed because there are a lot of women, with promising careers, in Jennifer's position.

Like Maud Gonne, although I wouldn't bet on the career. According to Jennifer, she forgot her diaphragm on a weekend trip to Stowe, Vermont, and that was that. Maud, on the other hand, might go out tonight to purchase one, given the circumstances, but I know for a fact that she's such a good girl, she would never have defied my mother by using birth control in the first place.

I don't exactly understand my mother. I've never pursued the subject to find out, fearing that she believes we are as innocent as she was at our age. But certainly when we have our Serious Discussions about Life Chance, it sounds very much as though she doesn't care what we do as long as we don't do it with birth control. I know for a fact that isn't true, but I bet it's the rationalization Maud used when she did it the first time.

Just last week Mother came home from the classes she gives at St. Jude's for young R.C. women on the rhythm method of birth control, which happens to be the only one advocated by Life Chance. She was full of didactic enthusiasm and she had the great luck to find Maud and me studying in the kitchen together—which is to say,

Maud was studying, I presume, and I had my literature book opened to *Paradise Lost* and was in the early stages of imagining a scene between me and a guy I'd seen at the drugstore on the couch in our recreation room.

"Do you understand the rhythm method?" she said, whirling into the kitchen with the drive of a coastal hurricane. She sat down between us at the kitchen table.

"I *love* Milton," she said, glancing at my literature book, opened to *Paradise Lost*. She has never, I am sure, read Milton but with a title like *Paradise Lost,* he sounds Christian, so she thinks she'd love him.

"I understand the rhythm method very well," I said. "If you don't screw, you don't get pregnant. It's a revolutionary discovery."

My mother's enthusiasm is interrupted for a moral consideration of my vocabulary, which includes one of the Oxford Unabridged's definitions of the word *screw*—which does not happen to reflect my use of it.

"It is perfectly possible to have a pleasurable sexual life with your husband and still use the rhythm method," my mother went on. She took out a notebook and drew a graph. "Let us say, for example, your period begins on the eighth of May," she said to Maud.

Maud looked painfully up from her book. It is difficult for me to say now whether the painful expression was a result of the fact that Mother had interrupted her reading of *Henry IV, Part II* or had reminded her that her period hadn't begun and wasn't likely to.

Mother charged ahead. "And is over on May thirteenth or fourteenth. These days," she said, marking the fifteenth, sixteenth, seventeenth, and eighteenth, "are safe. After that, you have to abstain because around two weeks after your period begins, you will ovulate. So to be very safe, you can't resume any activity until the end of May."

"Which gives you about six chances a month," I said, acknowledging to myself that at the moment six chances would be better than nothing.

"It depends on your circumstances," my mother said, marking the safe days for Maud with a red pencil as though this will be useful for her at this point. The R.C. women at St. Jude's must each have I.Q.'s of about 82.

"Are you suggesting Maud and I use rhythm now?" I asked.

"Of course not," my mother said. "I am telling you what I teach, and I feel responsible to prepare you for marriage which, as you know, my own mother did not do for me."

"That's a break, Mother," I said, "because I'm planning to get married in the next week and I need to plan ahead."

"To whom?" Eliot asked, emerging from the basement.

"To you, the love of my life," I said to Eliot, who pretended charmingly to get sick in the kitchen sink.

Maud obviously missed the safe days. Unlike my mother, she isn't of a temperament likely to keep graphs. I can imagine that my mother keeps a chart under the pillow and marks the days she makes love. It probably adds up to six a year, and my father reads the paper while she fills out the graph.

Now I wonder what my mother is going to do when she finds out that Maud was using the rhythm method just as she had been told to do.

It's too late, of course, but I'm sure my mother would have said, "Have the baby—I'll raise him," and my father would probably have been delighted to make Jonathan Nims marry Maud just to have a senator's child as a son-in-law. But you can bet on one thing: Nothing that Maud could do short of mass murder on M Street would upset my mother more than having an abortion.

I wonder if she has told.

She could, of course, get very sick and *have* to tell.

My feelings are complicated. Part of me is sympathetic to my poor foolish mother, fighting against birth control while her dutiful daughter, following her advice, gets pregnant and has to have an abortion.

And, of course, a part of me would like to see the whole thing blow up in their faces.

Either way I can't resist calling home. I wait until the kitchen is empty and the living room silent with members of the Death Group pretending to die, I presume, and then I call. My mother answers before the end of the first ring.

"Hello," she says breathlessly, as though someone has a gun to her head.

I hang up. I'm afraid she'll recognize my breathing.

She could be breathless because I have left—or she could be breathless because she's waiting for a call from the doctor about Maud. I know I'm going to have to call back.

The man who has come in the kitchen to make a telephone call seems to be already dead. He is thin and pale and wears a black turtleneck and trousers, in honor, I guess, of the occasion. He makes a telephone call to his mother. He looks too old to have a mother. Nevertheless, he has one with whom he is having a fight at the moment about spending the night in Silver Spring and still getting her to the podiatrist on time the next day. I read the beauty section of *Redbook,* which is on hair, not weight, for a change.

"Mothers!" he says when he hangs up.

"Yeah," I agree.

When he has left the kitchen, I call again. This time it rings three times before Maud answers it.

"Hello," she says in her sugar-cane voice.

I don't reply and I don't hang up.

"Hello," she says again.

"Are you there?" she asks. She sounds perfectly well. Not even upset.

She probably had the abortion and it went fine. Half an hour in the waiting room for her blood pressure to stabilize, and she went downstairs to the pharmacy with a prescription for a Size 70 Diaphragm. Mother will never know. Maud Leary was born lucky.

"Well, good-bye," she says, and I stand in the kitchen holding the telephone, whose line is dead.

5

A Historical Perspective

The problems with my mother started years before I can remember. It is my guess that one afternoon between Mass and laundry and children's formulas, she looked in my crib and thought to herself, "Flesh of my flesh, blood of my blood," for that's the way I imagine my mother thinks to herself. "It is my duty to God to make this child worthy of Him."

Worthiness was not a problem, of course, with Maud Gonne, who was born worthy and besides, looks like my father's family so my mother has never felt responsible for her in quite the same way. Nor for that matter did worthiness apply to Eliot, who was a boy and to be admired for this accomplishment alone. But I expect that every time my mother looked at me when I was small, she saw a reproduction of her former self and decided, with this new opportunity in the flesh, to make up for past sins.

Well, you can imagine my response. By the time I was ten, I was as efficient as a nuclear reactor. I operated entirely according to the rules of opposites. I didn't take great risks with personal safety, leaving that area of specialty to Eliot—who liked to cross streets without looking just to test God's love for children—but I countered every request with an act of defiance.

I learned to faint without provocation in Mass, to hide in the cubicle in the bathroom during catechism, and twice I was caught cheating in math class. In sixth grade my mother was called in to school by the nuns because I had arrived with a pillow stuck under my uniform-jumper telling my classmates that I was suddenly and inexplicably pregnant.

"Virgin birth," I confessed.

"Degrading the holiness of life," the sister said to my mother.

"The holiness of pillows," I said under my breath, and was sent home for three days to pray for forgiveness—which time I used to read in my room three *True Romance*s cover to cover.

Later that same year, when my mother took me, against my will, for my twice yearly Dutch bob that made me look like a square-headed boy, I dyed my hair crimson-red in the bathtub, a color which, in future washings, pales to a rare and offensive pink.

It was a full-time job growing up to resist my mother's plans for me. She is a powerful woman, and with a purpose she could steamroller a choir of angels if they were on the wrong course. I can imagine her as an early German warrior, crossing herself for hasty forgiveness every time she speared the enemy through the heart.

"Your mother is a well-meaning woman," my father tells me the few times I have complained to him. And I must confess, he is right. She may have squashed and smothered every cell in my brain, but she has done it out of Love and Concern. Her words, I should add.

"What I have done, Mary, is always out of Love and Concern," she says.

Dum-dum-de-dum-dum, Love and Concern. I've made up a short song about it.

I am not entirely stone-hearted about my mother. I can, for example, be moved by the stories of her childhood and early marriage, as long as I reflect on them in the privacy of my room and don't have to listen to them told to me in the kitchen as an excuse for her insistence on making a Wonderful Family while we both stuff ourselves with macaroons.

She was the last of nine children and the only girl, but she came too late after her mother's interest in girls had turned, around the sixth or seventh child, to dachshunds and rare parrots and painting still-life flower arrangements in a studio she leased. So Mother was raised by a nanny who died when she was seven and ignored by her brothers who, without exception, found her dispensable. It is not any wonder that she was, as she's said, "Very Unhappy."

And that is why she has devoted herself without relief to creating a Wonderful Family so we will not remember our childhoods as Very Unhappy. I can't fault her for that, but on the whole the family would have a better chance at happiness if Mother relaxed, and took a short-term vacation—maybe giving some thought to a trip to Venezuela, where she could sell Maud Gonne to a wealthy Latin landowner. I am not without hope, you see.

My mother met my father when she was eighteen and he was a clerk in her father's law firm. According to him, "Nora took my breath away." And I can understand that. Because of my mother's smothering, my lungs are probably one eighth the normal size of teenage lungs.

According to my mother, she married my father because he asked her to and because he was well educated, intelligent, and pleased her father, who was glad to be done with parental duties for good.

"When I married your father, I didn't know about making love," my mother told me. "Specifically," she often adds—and I guess she had imagined the white-knight-on-the-white-horse variety of making love—a vision that I gave up by the time I was eight years old, when Maud Gonne drew me an explicit diagram, complete with positions detailing how it could be done and forgetting the white horse.

"It was quite a shock to find out what was expected of me," my mother has said. My guess is, she believed Virgin birth was widespread.

My parents moved into the house in Georgetown where we now live, four blocks from her parents' house, one mile from Georgetown University Hospital, where she went by bus to give birth to her first child because my father was in Vietnam fulfilling his duty to his country. She named the first baby Andrew after he had died of hyaline membrane disease, and for weeks she could not write my father about this dead child because—so she has told Maud and me in earnest, I promise you—she was afraid that her innocence of sex had been responsible for the baby's death. I don't know what the Catholic Church would do to survive in the Western World were it not for guilt.

So there she was, nineteen years old with one dead baby, an absent husband, and an excess of God. She started going to Mass twice a day to keep from being lonely. She did good works in a Catholic charity-house downtown and slept alone at night with her childhood doll under her pillow, dreaming of babies. I am not making this up. Sometimes when I think about her then, I could weep—a condition always cut short by her arrival in the flesh in my room for a Serious Discussion or her strident voice responding to Aunt Ethel's criticism on the telephone or simply her face reflected when I look at myself in the mirror above my dresser.

When my father returned from Vietnam to practice law, Maud was born—her ankles slender at conception, no doubt—and my mother collected her insatiable energy and expended it on Maud Gonne. Life Chance didn't come into the picture until Mother was pregnant with me, and I was the child who needed the treatment with insatiable energy. Instead, two months and four days short of my birth, Mother was made secretary of the Washington chapter of Life Chance, and although I do not have any specific memory of that time, my unspecific memories show my mother on the telephone with a long yellow cord that allowed her to go from the kitchen to the living room, hand me a bottle, write some notes on a list on her desk, toss me soft toys to play with, and wash the vegetables for supper without a break in her ardent conversation. So much for a happy childhood.

I do not mean to pretend that I was the only family victim of Life Chance, because Mother was vice president of the Washington chapter by the time Eliot was born—but Eliot had all kinds of advantages as a boy and the youngest, and, as I have said, his requirements for happiness were less than mine. Witness him on the couch, smoking dope with Pauline! He had simple tastes from birth, and apparently my own love cup has a leak at the bottom, because all I have ever wanted is more.

My childhood was spent in the playroom of the house in winter, in the garden in summer, a routine interrupted once daily by a trip to the market at O Street, which was the general extent of my mother's excursions out of the house. Looking back, I think she had (maybe still has), a case of agoraphobia—a disease of the mind that makes one afraid to go far outside the house, because even now, in spite of one trip to Chicago for Life Chance and a trip to Bermuda forced on her by my father, my mother's relationships, business and personal, are carried on by telephone—one with a long cord. She has never, for example, been to a supermarket and, as far as I know, the farthest out of Georgetown she has been is National Cathedral School, which is twelve blocks north of our house. I doubt she has been across the river to Virginia since she was a little girl.

"Your mother is a born homebody," my father says with great pleasure, as though my mother's condition is a direct result of her love for him. He is, I have to admit, the sort of man who likes the fact that my mother's only contact with the outside world is safely via Ma Bell—unlike the mothers of some people at school, who are, according to their children, trysting in the Holiday Inn, Arlington, or at an apartment in Fairfax with members of their husbands' law firms or their statistics professors in graduate school.

I was a sweet child early on, contrary to later developments. There didn't seem to be a choice, or you can bet I would have chosen it. My mother was nonstop on the trail of saving fetuses; my father worked a twenty-three-hour day: full-time as a lawyer, full-time as a law professor, full-time as a member of any committee that asked him—so that's three full-time jobs—eight times three, give or take a little. And Maud Gonne was, on a full-time basis, not sweet. My first idea, though I was too young to articulate it, was that if I was sweet, people would love me. By the time I was six, I had realized, by comparing my rewards in life with those of Maud, that I had been in error. If I was sweet, people did not need to pay attention to me. Or worse, they could treat me badly.

At that same time, at Our Lady of Ladies, I had an Instructive Experience, as my mother called it, in the hands of Allison Shakey, God strike her dead. I was plump, not fat, with glasses. I believed in God and prayed for Him to forgive my many sins. To a certain extent I believed that the world was good because man was born good—thank you, Jean-Jacques Rousseau—only to be corrupted by society. I even believed that the people I liked would like me back, not equally perhaps, but I was, in my early childhood, accommodating by nature. I liked Allison Shakey. She was beautiful—with dimples, blue eyes, yellow curls—and, of course, skinny and without glasses. The nuns thought she was an angel accidentally dropped from heaven one afternoon to purify the depraved souls of children.

Little did they know. We were on the playground jumping rope, a sport which, given my thick legs, was not my long suit, when Allison Shakey, God strike her dead, asked me to turn around so my backside would be facing her.

"Why?" I asked, very mildly distrustful.

"Just turn around, Mary," she said.

"Yeah, go on," another girl said.

"Come on, Mary," someone else said.

"I won't do anything," Allison said with great sincerity.

So I turned around.

And of course, Allison kicked me so hard in the bottom that I fell over, skinning my knee, ripping my jumper at the waist, which had to be pinned back on me by Sister Grace so it wouldn't fall off that day, thereby giving the rest of the class a great deal of pleasure.

The sisters did not believe me.

"What did you do to provoke Allison?" Sister Grace asked.

"Nothing," I said.

And Sister Grace raised her tiny eyebrows and said, I presume, a few silent Hail Marys for me so I could be forgiven my lie about Angel Allison, God strike her dead again and again and again. Sister Grace as well, for that matter.

Which marked the end of my sweetness.

I metamorphosed the following day into a different level of animal life, and the rest of my schooldays until I was kicked out of Our Lady of Ladies were spent providing Sister Grace with the opportunity to say daily Hail Marys for me.

That also marked the beginning of my mother's all-out campaign to make me a worthy child of God.

6
Life Chance

Since I left Our Lady of Ladies under a cloud of black smoke, two years and nine months exactly to the day I left My Mother of Mothers for the Reverend and Dr. Page's, I have been the subject for every serious reform my mother considers "Useful"—her word—except Life Chance.

She believes, poor demented soul, that by bearing me, she has given me the Life Chance while I struggle for air under the weight of her good intentions. Some life chance.

My first idea, as I have said, after I left Our Lady of Ladies, was to lose my virginity. National Cathedral School has a boys' school called St. Alban's across the road, and it was my hope that the boys at St. Alban's had heard of my expulsion from

Our Lady of Ladies and would consider me an easy woman. I planned, in fact, to be easy when the opportunity arose. I dreamed about it at night when I couldn't sleep owing to anxieties and to listening to Maud Gonne sleeping like a lamb in the room next to mine. I even, poor fool that I was, began to copy the methods invented by Maud Gonne for entrapping males. I noticed that she always carried a lot of useless books in her backpack to appear burdened, that she walked with her head tilted toward the sky, and that she assumed a look of tragic abstraction when a boy walked by.

"What's the matter, Maud?" the boy would probably say.

"Oh, n-n-nothing," Maud would reply in a voice that suggested there had been two unexpected deaths and a diagnosis of liver cancer in her immediate family alone.

I unfortunately do not have the face for trage-dy. In fact, it is a round face with freckles and a mouth that turns slightly up even if I've taped it for a sullen expression. If I were to say "Oh, nothing" in Maud's voice, the boy would laugh, give a fake box to the upper arm, and say something reassuring like, "You'd make a wonderful nun, Mary."

It is impossible for me to believe, given the general turmoil in my belly, that I give off, like a frightened animal, the odor of celibacy, but from the response at St. Alban's I evidently do.

I even went so far as to engage Maud in a

personal discussion in her bedroom while I watched her try her hair in Victorian styles for the St. Alban's Senior Prom.

"When did you start going out?" I began casually enough.

"Seventh grade," she said, examining her hair at the side with a hand mirror. "You know, seriously —in seventh grade."

I *didn't* know, for chrissake. That was the whole point of the humiliating conversation; but I didn't let on to Maud. Instead, I leaned back against her headboard and tried on an expression of boredom.

"You mean, started kissing and stuff," I said.

"Oh, that was in sixth," she said.

I had a sudden vision of Maud at twelve, without breasts to speak of, in one of the positions she had drawn for me when I was eight years old. This conversation was way above my head. No wonder I had run into difficulty.

"So what do you do now?" I asked.

"Do?" She was taking her hair down and brushing it into another style.

"You know, with boys," I said.

Maud was in eleventh grade at the time, and Jonathan Nims was just one of the boys who came over to see her on weekends.

"Like Jonathan," I added.

"Sort of what I feel like," she said matter-of-factly.

Well, I knew what I felt like, and if she felt the

same way with all those opportunities to act on, I was dumbstruck with admiration. It was a wonder that she had time for homework.

"Who do you like?" she asked me—kindly, I should say.

"Oh, anyone," I said with great innocence, but the fact was, I meant it—anyone would do.

Which is how, at the beginning of my sophomore year, I happened to meet Jack Richards, who did not go to St. Alban's or, for that matter, to school at all unless you call Hillsdale House for the Reformation of Delinquent Boys a school.

In early November, a Tuesday after piano, I got on the B34, which goes down Wisconsin Avenue to Georgetown, and all of the seats were taken except the ones in the front reserved for senior citizens. There's still enough of the Catholic girls' school training imprinted in indelible ink on my brain to keep me from sitting in the senior citizens seats, so I stood at the front of the bus and held on to the bar. Jack Richards got on at the second stop, right in front of Hillsdale House. He had an unlit cigarette between his teeth, his hair was parted in the middle, and he had bands around the sleeves of his pin-striped shirt like the ones I've seen in pictures of my grandfather. No coat.

"Toss the cigarette, buddy," the bus driver said.

"I'm pleased to oblige you," Jack Richards said pleasantly, and leaned out the open window beside me, flicking the cigarette onto Wisconsin Avenue.

Then he sat down in one of the seats reserved for senior citizens and smiled at me.

"Sit," he said. "There's plenty of room."

"I'd rather stand," I said. "I've been sitting all day." I certainly wasn't going to pass moral judgment when my poor heart was beating like crazy in my temples.

He leaned his head back against the leather seat, closed his eyes halfway, and looked at me through the slits.

"Catholic school?" he asked, eyeing my uniform, the aqua plaid pleated skirt adding a square foot to my hips.

"Nope. Cathedral School."

"I used to go to Catholic school," he said. "Until May of last year, when I was expelled."

Common ground, I thought with trembling excitement. I moved closer, so the gray-haired woman who worked in the Lower School at Cathedral and was sitting in the first row could not hear me.

"Me too," I said.

He smiled at me, and I swear, he moved his knee on purpose just slightly so it touched my left leg.

"What for?" he asked.

"Smoking," I said.

"Mine was for stealing cars," he said. "And other things."

"Worse?" I asked with clear admiration.

He shrugged. "It depends entirely on individual judgment what is bad and what is worse."

The bus was coming to my stop. I considered staying on to M Street, on the pretense of shopping. Perhaps, I thought, I could go to the end of the line or get off where he did, saying, "What a coincidence!"

But, as it happened, I remembered my thick legs, my round and freckled face, my tortoiseshell glasses, and dismissed future possibilities with the boy from Hillsdale.

"My stop," I said. "See you."

I put my hand on the railing to steady myself as the bus careened down Wisconsin Avenue toward R and the boy got up from the senior citizens seat and put his hand on top of mine.

Well, I nearly died on the spot. Cardiac arrest at fifteen and three quarters.

"Mine too," he said in my ear. I promise. He was so close, he could have kissed me.

That comes later. But don't get your hopes up for a happy ending, like I did.

"Where are you going?" I asked. "To the library?"

I had to say something, but, as you can well imagine, Jack Richards was not the sort of boy you'd expect to see in the Georgetown Branch Library across the street from my house.

"Not the library," he said, laughing, and took out a cigarette, offering me one. "Smoke?"

"Nope," I said.

"Dope, ever?" he asked.

"Sure," I said, which was the first of a history of lies that grew like weeds in the short time I knew Jack Richards. "But not now," I added.

"Where are you going?" he asked.

"Home," I said.

"You live in Georgetown?" He raised his eyebrows. "Fancy." He whistled.

"No, we're pretty poor," I said.

"Yeah, I bet."

"Honest," I said. "We're the poorest on our block."

"I'll walk you home," he said.

We exchanged names. I said mine was Shannon Leary. Honest to God, I do not know why I did that but I did. Mary sounded like the name of a virgin and Shannon like the name of an unreformed prostitute, so I took my chances.

Jack said his father had died in an elevator accident when he was four. He had fallen down the shaft. He had one brother who died at birth, and thereafter his mother was infertile, so there were no more offspring, which was a good thing because his mother developed a rare blood disease and was bedridden. Even Charles Dickens would have had trouble making up such a tragic story.

"My God," I kept saying.

"Other people I know have it much worse," he said against my protests.

I invited him to move in with us, and he refused

on the grounds that he had to spend the next four years in reform school. It wasn't bad, he said. In fact, the meals were the best he'd ever had. Besides, he got to leave three afternoons a week to visit his infant son, born to the girl he got pregnant when he was in the ninth grade at Catholic school.

"So you're a father," I said.

He nodded. "And only fifteen."

He looked thirty-seven.

"You're sure you're fifteen?"

"I'll be sixteen December one," he said. I could see one missing tooth close to the front of his mouth when he smiled.

He told me he thought I'd look pretty in different clothes. Maybe a black dress, he suggested. Or even corduroys. I tried to remember the last time I'd looked at myself in the mirror. He was, I decided, an optimist.

When Maud came home from school, I was trying on a black dress of my mother's that she had gotten for Granny's funeral and had worn to Aunt Jen's and Father Patrick's funerals as well. To my horror it did not zip at the waist.

"You might try the water diet," Maud said by mistake while she watched me trying to zip Mother's dress. Without another word I picked the Scope up off the sink, walked in Maud's room, and poured it on her lavender-flowered quilt. Later, of course, I had to change her bed, wash the quilt, and air out the mattress, but on the whole, revenge is often worth the price.

The following day I went on the water diet. The water diet consists of eight glasses of water, a hard-boiled egg for breakfast, cottage cheese for lunch, and a steak for dinner.

"I'll buy my own steak," I said when my mother protested. By the third day I had lost four pounds, and Mother was beginning to assume an attitude of serious alarm.

"I have a friend whose daughter has anorexia," my mother said as I ate my steak on the third night.

"Not a chance," I said. "I'm not the anorectic type."

"She nearly died," she said. "She may still."

In the mirror on Maud's door, with nothing on, I still looked exactly the same front-on and side-ways. *Fat.*

"No, you're not," my mother said.

"Mary's stocky," Eliot said.

"Handsome," my father said in a rare compliment.

"Which would be swell if I were going to grow up to be a man," I said.

Maud said nothing.

By the fifth day my mother was hysterical.

"Please, Mary," she begged.

I promised to stop at seven days.

The fact is, as I've learned by now, my mother wants me to be fat to keep her company. I suppose she'd feel the same way if she had a harelip or one leg. And I have always been under the misapprehension that in America parents want a better life for their children than they had. The sociologists haven't met my mother.

"Have you met some boy?" Maud asked.

"Nope," I replied.

"If you lose any more weight," Eliot said on the fifth day, "you'll be flat-chested."

It was Maud who answered the phone when Jack Richards called. We were in the kitchen getting dinner ready, since Mother had a Life Chance Convention at the Washington Hilton and Maud grabbed the phone, expecting—with good reason —that the call was for her.

"Shannon," she said. "No, I think you have the wrong number."

I practically killed myself trying to get to the phone. I fell over a kitchen chair, got my foot caught in the bottom rung, and twisted my ankle.

"Apparently Shannon has just materialized. Here," she said, tossing the phone at me. "Take it."

I was too out of breath to talk. He asked me to go to Dumbarton Oaks for a picnic on Saturday, and I said I thought I could. He asked me to make the picnic, and said he'd pick me up at noon.

"Who was that?" Maud asked.

"A friend," I replied.

"So you told him your name was Shannon Leary," she said. "Not a bad name."

I snapped the ends of the string beans and washed the lettuce for salad.

"Lucky you were here when I answered, or he never would have found you."

I set the table and put out the glasses.

"What's he like?" Maud asked, checking the meat loaf.

"I hate the name Mary," I said, and went to my room.

By Friday my mother had found out everything about Jack Richards. That he was in Hillsdale House for stealing cars, vandalizing, and breaking and entering houses in Cleveland Park. Don't ask me how she did it. She ought to consider joining the FBI, where her work would be appreciated. I told her his name and that I'd met him on a bus and which Catholic school he had gone to—except I said he was still there. I should have known better. My mother has a remarkable capacity for invading my life, and I ought to make a regular practice of lying.

"So I suppose I can't go on the picnic," I said.

"Not at all," my mother said. "I just want to meet him. Have him come here first."

"So you can give him the third degree?"

"So I can meet him," she said very kindly.

"And then follow us to Dumbarton Oaks, I suppose, so he won't murder me."

"Not at all, Mary."

"I don't believe you," I said.

I could tell she had a plan.

Jack Richards arrived early on Saturday. I was in my bedroom with a towel around my waist, trying to decide which pair of underwear would show less under my white painter's pants, when Eliot knocked and said sweetly, "The convict has arrived."

I should have known then not to leave my mother alone with him for a second—I should have gone immediately downstairs in my towel. But instead, vanity of vanities, I had to blow-dry my hair. My hair, at a certain length that is never allowed for long, is my best feature. I put on a black turtleneck that disguises the fact that I don't have a neck, a little of Maud's peach blush-on, and perfume. I have this thing about perfume. If all else fails, as it usually does, at least I can smell good.

By the time I go downstairs, Mother has taken Jack in the kitchen, set him at the table with a plate of oatmeal-raisin cookies she has made to fatten me up again, and is about to swallow him whole when I walk in.

"Hi," I said.

"Jack and I have been having a good talk about the church," she said.

"I was raised Catholic," he said, as though they'd just made a decision to go to Mass together.

"I don't want to keep you," Mother said, getting up from the kitchen table.

"Aren't you coming?" I asked with a large dose of sarcasm when she handed me the picnic basket of sandwiches she had made.

"Sure. Why don't you," Jack said as if he honestly meant it.

Mother declined with great sincerity. She said she had work to do.

"On Life Chance," I said with evil intent, thinking certainly any fifteen-year-old juvenile-delinquent father would bomb the Life Chance headquarters, given half a chance. Wrong again.

"I like your mother a lot," he said as we went through the gates of Dumbarton Oaks. "She's a terrific woman."

I had the afternoon carefully imagined. It included eating a picnic near the farthest northwest corner of Dumbarton Oaks, where people seldom go, while we talked about love, death—crime, certainly—and maybe sex. It included me leaning against a dogwood tree so my face fell in shadows. In semidarkness, my hair in soft curls around my face, I would look thinner. Jack would lean over and kiss me on the lips, holding his lips to mine for a long time. These imaginings did not include my mother. But she may just as well have come along.

We ate lunch in the isolated northwest corner of the gardens. When I brought up the subject of love and death, he changed the subject of the conversation to what my mother had said in the kitchen about the Catholic Church, as if it were of passionate interest to us both. The talk about crime had to do with my mother's compassion for criminals. I did not bring up the subject of sex. First I tried leaning against a tree and then lying down slightly on my side in what I thought was a position of provocation.

I should mention, as if you don't already know, that he was not without sense in matters of sex. He knew what I was up to.

"Listen, Shannon," he said finally. "I can't kiss you."

What I should have said was "Thank God. I was hoping you couldn't."

But instead, I said, "Why not?"

He shook his head sadly.

"You're a nice girl, Shannon. I just can't."

"You wouldn't have to do anything else," I said.

I couldn't believe my own voice. I had lost all sense of pride. I scrambled to a sitting position and began packing away the remains of the picnic.

"Your mother'd kill me if I kissed you," he said.

You can imagine how well the rest of the afternoon went. Jack Richards walked me home at four o'clock and said good-bye and that he'd call me sometime, but I knew perfectly well, as he walked down R Street, he was leaving my life forever.

"What did you say to him?" I asked my mother fiercely after she had hung up with Aunt Ethel.

"Nothing in particular. We had a very nice talk," my mother said.

"I bet," I said.

Later Eliot told me.

Mother, he said, was sitting next to Jack just as I started to come downstairs from the third floor in my perfume and blush-on and black turtleneck.

"Take good care of her," Mother said to the convict, gripping his hands as though the armies of Dionysus were going to strip me naked in Dumbarton Oaks. "She's never been out on a date before."

Eliot was making lemonade and overheard the whole thing.

So you begin to see the extent of my mother's obligation to make me a worthy child of God.

7
Life As a
Runaway

I am lying in bed in a small room at the top of the back stairs in the Pages' house. It has one window without blinds directly opposite a streetlight. It is the cats' room. There are at the moment two cats on my bed and three cats positioned other places in the room, plus a cardboard kitty litter box that hasn't been emptied for some time. I have opened the window, but the night is too still for ventilation —in fact, a tornado would be necessary to air out this room. One of the cats, a black one with only one ear, has moved up on my pillow to manicure its claws. I don't need to tell you that I can't sleep.

Downstairs the Death Group is breaking up. They are trying to decide whether to take their caskets, since they plan to meet again tomorrow night. By the clatter in the front hall I guess they have decided in favor of keeping their caskets close at hand, for which I am grateful. On the whole I would prefer it if the Reverend Page involved himself in Sex Groups as long as I am living here.

Now the Pages are having a fight in the kitchen. I can't hear his voice, but so far she has called him "weak" and "incompetent" and another word, which I will leave out. It doesn't seem to bother them that several members of the Death Group are still in the front hall. Or that I'm upstairs.

"I'm sleeping in my casket tonight," the Reverend Page says distinctly.

"Just where you belong," Sally Page replies. She comes up the back stairs, into my room, and turns on the light. It is the first I've seen of her since I arrived.

"Asleep?" she asks very pleasantly, just as I remember her.

"No, not yet."

"I remember you now," she says. "You came up to me after a talk I gave at Georgetown last month."

I am happy and surprised to be memorable in a crowd until I remember that it is probably because of my hips.

"Billy says you've come to stay for the summer, which is just wonderful. You can start off tomorrow immediately by giving the children breakfast. I have to be at a seminar first thing, and Billy sleeps late."

She tells me about the other people in the house—the woman minister responsible for the Reverend Page's unemployment and Zeke, Sally Page's brother, who is painting the house in exchange for room and board.

"Don't worry about Billy and me fighting," she said. "We do it all the time." She smiles and kisses me good night as if we've been friends for years. Just before she turns out the light, she brushes the one-eared cat off my bed with a civilized gesture.

At three o'clock in the morning—I know the time because I go downstairs and check the illuminated clock in the kitchen—I am still awake. So far I have blamed the cats, the streetlights shining in my eyes, the casket holding the sleeping Reverend Billy Page, but the fact is, every time I close my eyes, the head of my mother—mermaid fashion, half a body and no legs, floats into view, and sits without mercy inside my closed eyelids.

I imagine the scene at dinner tonight with our Wonderful Family minus me.

"Mary's gone," Eliot says, emerging red-eyed from the basement. "Run away. She told me so." He sinks into a kitchen chair and contemplates the granules of sugar in the sugar bowl.

"Of course, she hasn't," my mother says with false confidence. "She's in a bad humor. She'll be back."

"So what?" Maud says, if she's home from the hospital in time for dinner. She is probably cooking beans and slicing tomatoes, good-girl fashion, so no one will suspect her of criminal involvement.

"Well, that's what she told me," Eliot says slowly. "And you know Mary."

"What about Mary?" my mother asks with an edge of panic in her voice.

"S-t-u-b-b-o-r-n," Eliot says, spelling it. In some ways Eliot hasn't advanced much beyond second grade.

"Maudie, would you check some of Mary's friends to see if she's visiting?"

"Yeah, visiting," Eliot says, sticking a wet finger in the sugar bowl and licking the coating slowly.

Maud calls Katie Aster, Ann Fry, and Pamela Flower, and all of them are studying for their U.S. history exam and haven't seen me since the French exam that morning.

My father is sitting in the garden next to the statue of St. Michael, reading the editorial page of *The Washington Post.* He does not stop reading when my mother comes out to tell him that supper is ready and I have disappeared. Maybe, if she is to believe Eliot, I have run away.

He finishes Al Hess's column, folds the paper neatly in fours, open to the two editorials he has not read, and comes in for supper.

My mother believes in eating in the dining room at dinner—with napkins and candles—the meal, served from the head of the table, sitting there getting cold while we say grace. Tonight Mother gives the grace. She adds bravely that she hopes God will see fit to return me to them soon, and in the meantime, she hopes I will see the Light. I've never been sure what the Light is, but in our communal prayers, Mother is always requesting that one or the other of us sees it. I suppose when if ever it comes, I'll know it.

Eliot says I have run away because I don't get along with Mother.

Maud says that I am ungrateful and insecure— the latter her favorite word this year—and that I have taken all of her best underwear.

My father says he is going to call the police.

My mother objects, saying the police will make it a public affair, and, of course, I'll be back and she would die of humiliation if anything were printed in the newspapers.

"Daughter Runs Away from Home Due to Anger at Mother," Eliot says, helpfully inventing headlines.

My father calls the police. "This," he points out to my mother, "is what the police are for."

After dinner Eliot goes downstairs to the base- ment to smoke more dope in front of the television. Maud does the dishes, sweeps the floor and back steps, changes to a lavender dress that shows her nipples, kisses Mother and Father good-bye, and goes off to Tracey Place, her new diaphragm in place. Of course, I haven't any idea about the effects of an abortion so it may be she's only up to French-kissing tonight.

Mother and Father and the police sit in the living room—Mother pretending it's a social occasion, serving coffee in demitasse cups. My father gives a thorough description of me and several suggestions of where I might have gone. To Philadelphia where my grandmother lives. To Batavia, New York, where I have an old camp friend. To Esther, Wyoming, where his brother has a ranch. He calls Esther while the police are still there, and his brother says he'll call straightaway if I arrive.

After the police leave, my parents sit together in the living room without talking. At one in the morning Eliot comes upstairs after *The Late Movie* and they are still sitting in the living room. At two in the morning Maud arrives in a rumpled lavender dress, kisses my mother and father good night, and goes upstairs to dream about herself as Joan of Arc.

At three in the morning I call. My heart is beating like a band in my temples. I don't know what to expect when my mother answers the telephone—I suppose that she will float magically through the wires and swallow me whole while I stand, unsuspecting, in the Pages' kitchen.

"I am perfectly safe," I say quickly. "I'll let you know tomorrow by letter where I am," I say, and hang up.

I can see her at the other end. She replaces the receiver on the hook and sits down in the cane chair beside the phone. "Hail, Mary, Mother of God, et cetera, et cetera, et cetera," she whispers.

I am free, I think, tiptoeing across the kitchen floor. Free, free, free. I creep past the casket with the Reverend Page, up the steps.

"So you ran away from home," the Reverend Page says perfectly clearly from his casket.

I almost jump out of my skin.

He sits up, and I can see by the streetlight he is fully dressed.

"I could tell when you came this evening that you were in trouble."

"How could you tell?" I whisper.

"Just a look about you," he says.

Two bits he's going to tell me tomorrow morning that God told him. And if that's so, after exams I'm moving to an Indian reservation where they still worship the sun and thunderstorms and witch doctors.

"Good night," he calls after me.

"Good night," I say.

I move the one-eared cat off my pillow, the golden cat off the center of my bed, and fall into a deep sleep from which I am startled awake in the pitch-dark by a child straddling my belly and saying directly into my face, "Are you awake?"

8
Zeke and Other Possibilities

I have neglected to mention to Sally Page that I have a U.S. history exam at National Cathedral School at one o'clock. It's eight thirty in the morning, and we are sitting at the breakfast table eating dry cornflakes and powdered juice.

"Every time Billy's Death Group comes, they finish all the milk and orange juice," she says lightly, as though it doesn't bother her a bit to eat cereal dry.

I have been up since five, when Cassie climbed on my stomach. I have washed the kitchen floor, fed the twins, and redone the dishes in the dishwasher because they looked dirty when I took them out. That is something my mother would do, I thought as I S.O.S.-ed plates crusted with food to satisfy the Cleanliness-is-next-to-godliness line of thought.

Sally Page is giving me, off the top of her head, a list of things to do. I am soon to learn that most things come from off the top of Sally Page's head. The twins can go to the park, she says, and Albert will be back from his grandmother's at noon.

"Don't let Albert upset you," she says. This is the second piece of bad news I have had about Albert. Could I go to the store and stock up on staples? she adds, handing me a signed blank check. I presume I look like the sort of young woman who knows what staples are, so I hesitate to ask her to be more specific. If there is an emergency, a real emergency, she adds—life-and-death variety (already I am imagining with very little trouble that variety of emergency)—I can have her paged at the conference. She writes the number of the conference room down on the other side of the check.

"What about the Reverend Page?" I ask rather foolishly.

"Billy?" she throws up her hands. "He'll be in and out, I suppose."

She gets up, grabs her briefcase, kisses the twins on the cheek and me on the head, and dashes out the back door.

"Don't, for heaven's sake, let Zeke offend you," she calls to me. "See you at six."

"Zeke dead?" Cassie asks happily from her high chair.

"Zeke fat?" Thomas asks.

"Beats me," I say.

I never asked Dr. Page about the U.S. history exam, I think as I rinse the dishes. Perhaps I could call in sick. After all, I haven't exactly studied for the exam. Or maybe the Reverend Page can take care of the children while I take the exam. That is, if he ever wakes up between his Death Group meetings.

"Cassie eat," Thomas says, pulling at my blue-jean pocket.

I look down. Cassie has gotten down from her high chair and is sitting on the floor next to the cat food bowl, stuffing her cheeks with cat food.

"Cassie, no," I say. "Spit it out."

She shakes her head and picks up another small kernel of dry cat food, trying to stick it in my mouth.

"No," I say loudly. She is shaking her head back and forth.

"Please spit it out," I say. "You could choke." Already a life-and-death emergency, and it's only eight forty-five.

Thomas spills the remaining cat food on the floor and runs with the cat food bowl into the living room.

"Please, Cassie."

She has stopped shaking her head. I think she is going to spit the cat food out.

"That's a good girl," I say, full of hope, and she does spit the cat food out—directly at me—in my face, my hair, and down my shirt.

"Cassie!" I shout.

The Reverend Billy Page walks in the kitchen holding Thomas's hand.

"We try not to shout at the children," he says in a very pleasant voice. I brush the cat food off my shirt and out of my hair.

"Help Mary, Cassie," he says sweetly, and kisses Thomas's head. "Daddy's going to get a little more sleep. He was up very late. Did Sally tell you about the park?" he asks me.

I nod. I consider telling him about my exam, but I can tell this is not the appropriate time.

I have cleaned the last piece of cat food off, filled the cats' bowl, and am about to pick up the twins from the kitchen floor, where they are crayoning in red directly on the linoleum, when Zeke comes teetering down the back stairs in silver strap-sandals, a short-haired blond wig, and a red taffeta evening gown.

"Zeke dead," Cassie says happily from the floor.

"No, baby," Zeke says, pinching her plump cheek. "Zeke is very much alive. That's Daddy's game. Daddy plays dead." He opens the refrigerator and takes out two hot dogs.

"Carcinogens," he says to me, as though we meet this way every morning. "I only eat cancer-causing foods. Coffee ready?" he asks. He drops the hot dogs in a pan of gray water on the stove and turns on the gas.

"Daddy dead?" Cassie asks.

"Their father is into death right now," Zeke says. "He wants us all to be comfortable with dying, so we talk about it all the time around here. It gives him a real charge."

"Zeke pretty," Thomas says, pulling on the red taffeta skirt.

"You think so, Thomas?" He takes one hot dog out of the water, shaking it to cool it off.

"I went to a masquerade ball last night as a woman and slept in my clothes. I am," he says, bowing, then taking my hand and kissing the tips of my fingers, "really a man."

"I guessed it," I say.

"My name is Zeke."

"Sally told me about you. I'm Mary Leary."

He looks at me with great seriousness.

"You look like a painting by Rubens. I love round women." He blows me a kiss. "I'm going to call you Sophette."

I pick up Cassie to leave for the park. She arches her back, digging her small feet into my stomach and pulling my hair.

"You'll find them charming children," Zeke says with sympathy. "Wait'll you meet Albert."

"I've been warned," I say.

"Albert bites," Thomas says.

"Wonderful," I say.

"So, Sophette, you are here to take care of the children for the summer while my sister advances her career and my brother-in-law accustoms himself to the condition of death by sleeping in a casket."

"It sounds a little creepy."

"It is. Since we have eternity to spend in our caskets, it's a little creepy to push your luck. I've decided I'll leave this place the first time I have the desire to spend the night in a casket. It's a good rule of thumb."

I take Thomas's hand and start out of the kitchen.

"You know," Zeke says pleasantly. "You ought to wear dresses. Your hips are too big for jeans. Good hips, though. Don't get me wrong."

He pinches off a piece of hot dog and puts it in Thomas's mouth.

"I'm taking them to the park. I'll see you later," I say.

I am halfway down the back steps when I make a connection between Zeke and my U.S. history exam. Zeke is eating a whole tomato with peanut butter when I get back to the kitchen.

"Listen," I say, "I have a terrible problem."

"I hate problems," he says.

"I have a final history exam at one today and am supposed to be taking care of the children at the same time," I say, undeterred.

He examines the tomato for bruises.

"I get the picture," he says, adjusting his blond wig so it covers part of his forehead and reveals his own dark blond straight hair in the back. "Does this include Albert?"

"He gets home at noon."

"Saint Peter and Saint Michael," he says, and throws this head back, closing his eyes. "You will owe me *something* for this one."

"Anything," I say. "I'll be in real trouble if I miss this exam."

"Anything?" he asks. "That's three hours of Albert. I'll consider the price."

We agree that I'll leave at twelve thirty and be back at four.

"I'd never do this for anyone else, Sophette," he says with mock passion, and kisses the ends of my fingers again.

It takes half an hour to walk the twins the block and a half to the Macomb Street playground, where I join a number of Spanish-speaking housekeepers and their charges in the sandbox. I think about Zeke while I build a castle for Thomas, which he knocks down before I have made the moat. I wonder if sometime later in the summer perhaps, after we have met daily in the kitchen as we have today, Zeke will stop me on the dark back stairs and kiss me on the lips in a gesture of love.

9
Surprise Reunion

I should have known that the mother of our Wonderful Family would be sitting outside Mr. Owens's U.S. history classroom, second floor back, when I walk out at three o'clock after flunking the examination. I was, to begin with, fifteen minutes late because Zeke twisted his ankle walking in the silver sandals.

"I wondered if you were planning to take the exam or not, Mary," Mr. Owens said to me.

I could have said, "I wasn't planning to, but there was nothing better to do this afternoon." But I don't say anything. Certainly not "Sorry I'm late."

I take an exam sheet, three blue books, and sit down in the back of the room behind Thunder Thighs, who is captain of the hockey team and sufficiently larger than I am to provide shelter from Mr. Owens.

Mr. Owens and I don't get along. He has made the usual observations about the fact that I don't live up to my potential, but he has added some more personal notes. He told my father that he found me surly and intellectually pretentious. He told my mother that he found me sanctimonious. I looked that one up. It means "holier than thou," which I am not. But my mother was pleased. Understanding students is not among Mr. Owens's few virtues.

I have a D-minus average going into the exam, with an Incomplete on my term paper entitled "The Role of Black Women in Nineteenth-Century American Society." I have until the end of this week to complete the paper, which, according to Mr. Owens, is not properly documented—a rare occasion on which he has been absolutely right.

"Incomplete, Mary," he said aloud when he handed out the rough drafts last week. "I hope you will learn that there are no Incompletes in life." That is the most profound observation he has made in the course of the year, and he makes it every time he gives an Incomplete.

Once Julie Brewster said, when her Incomplete was returned, "I thought this *was* life."

"This is school," Mr. Owens said with great

earnestness. "Which, you will find, is quite different from life."

By two o'clock I know I'm going to flunk the examination. I am thinking of Zeke in his red taffeta gown. I have to read the essay questions more than once because I can't concentrate. "Discuss the economic conditions that lead up to the Great Depression, using specific examples."

I think of writing: "The Depression was an invented phenomenon imagined by historians as a means of protecting the American people from the dangers of inflation. Just as Jesus Christ was invented to protect the people of Israel from the dangers of lust, greed, evil, blah blah blah."

I can't think of sensible answers to anything. By two thirty I am no longer concerned with whether or not I know any material. I simply want to answer every question, fill up the three blue books with writing that is illegible, on the off chance that Mr. Owens will be too tired and say to himself while he is correcting my exam, "I cannot read this examination paper. I'll just pass her so I never have to see her in class again."

Wishful thinking, of course. There's a whole essay question, counting thirty points, on the Taft-Hartley Act. I don't even remember what that act was. At three o'clock I finish the third book, stack the books together with my name on each one, and hand them in to Mr. Owens.

"Did you pass, Mary?" he asks with his usual kindness.

"I'm sure I did," I say brashly. "It wasn't all that difficult."

On the way out of the room I realize I made the wrong move. I should have crawled up to his desk, wet-eyed, and whispered, "Please, Mr. Owens, don't flunk me."

As you can imagine, I am in no mood to see my mother sitting in a folding chair just to the side of the classroom door, carefully placed so I cannot possibly see her and possibly fly out the window before she has a chance to catch me.

"Mary." She grabs me by the hand.

She is in the outfit she wears to see the priest. Blouse buttoned up to the neck, navy blue skirt, navy blue heels, and nylons. I expect she has seen him already today. Maybe twice. It is probably his idea that she hide out and wait for me.

I think of several escapes. I could run, of course. I could knock my mother to the ground, shouting, "NUCLEAR ATTACK!" and escape while she scrambles to her feet. I could fall apart in the corridor screaming, "Wash the blood off my hands!" and be carted away to St. Elizabeth's. I could faint. I might even, with a great effort, be able to foam at the mouth.

Unfortunately I cannot do any of these.

"Hello, Mother," I say. I presume she can hear my heart beating in my throat.

"Oh, Mary, I was so worried." She attempts to hug me. I don't embarrass her in front of the girls walking out of the U.S. history exam by saying, "Don't touch me," but I'm not pliable either.

"What are you doing now?" she asks. "Maybe we could go have tea."

"Tea?" I say. We have never gone out for tea before.

She smiles at Mr. Owens when he comes out and cannot resist saying that she disapproved of *Civil Disobedience* being on the history book list, which, I am sure, increases Mr. Owens's affection for me. I consider, as an alternative, saying to Mr. Owens that my mother disapproves of all U.S. history since the Revolution and therefore burned the text and all accompanying primary material by the statue of St. Michael in our backyard. Thus, my F in the exam.

"I don't think I have time for tea," I say to my mother. "I have a job."

She does not flinch. She doesn't ask me what job. She takes me by the elbow, as though we are intimate, and leads me to the car parked in the slot reserved for the chaplain.

"I'll drive you to your job," she says. "We need to have a Serious Discussion first."

I am not surprised by the mention of a Serious Discussion, of course, and climb in the car.

Once in the car I impress myself with my cool, reasonable, detached approach to alternatives. I could listen to her Serious Discussion and bolt in the middle. I could pretend to listen and think of Zeke. I could tell her I'd fallen in love with a boy who wore dresses. I could tell her the truth. Which I do.

We are driving along Wisconsin Avenue toward Georgetown when I say, "I honestly have a job for the whole summer and I'm not coming home until fall."

"Why didn't you tell me yesterday afternoon when we were talking," she says quite reasonably.

"Because I didn't get the job until last night."

"I value honesty above all," my mother says. She is traveling Wisconsin Avenue at about fifteen miles an hour in the left lane, as though she is about to turn, and people are beginning to honk.

"I am being honest. I'm telling you I have moved into the house with a family and I'm taking care of the children for the summer while the mother teaches summer school at Georgetown University. You know her."

"I know her?"

"You've met her."

"Where?"

"At Georgetown. She was making a speech."

My mother doesn't say anything. I can tell she is beginning to remember Sally Page. She has come to a complete stop on Wisconsin Avenue.

"If you don't drive, Mother, we're going to die on Wisconsin Avenue," I say.

She turns onto Calvert Street, pulls to the curb, and turns off the ignition. I am not prepared for a Serious Discussion at the beginning of rush hour in ninety-degree heat on Calvert Street.

I look over at my mother. She has her hand across her chest in a gesture of either patriotism or a heart-attack check. I have never thought that one could *will* paleness, but she is pale. I don't think of my mother as a woman who would collapse at bad news, but I am beginning to wonder if I have misjudged her.

"Are you okay?" I ask in spite of myself.

My mother doesn't say *anything*. In my conscious memory I cannot recall a time when my mother hasn't been talking.

"Are you sure you're okay," I say, a little worried, although she hasn't responded.

"Where does this woman live?" she asks finally.

I give her the address on Newark Street and she drives down Calvert to New Mexico, the long way around, although she certainly doesn't choose the long way to have more time to talk to me. She isn't talking to me at all.

At the light at Wisconsin and Macomb, she asks if Dr. Page is married or divorced. She says the word *divorced* as though it is synonymous with *murder*.

"Married," I say. "Her husband is an unemployed minister." I do not add anything about the Death Group. "That's why Sally Page has to work so hard to support the whole family."

My mother doesn't respond with sympathy.

When we get to Newark, I point out the house, and my mother stops the car. I am sorry to see that Zeke is on the front porch in blue jeans without a shirt. He is still wearing the blond wig like a hat on the back of his head, and he is carrying Cassie.

"Hello, beautiful Sophette," he calls from the porch. "Am I ever glad to see you."

"That's Zeke," I say to my mother. "He is Sally Page's brother," I add to his visible list of accomplishments.

"Does he live here?" she asks.

"Yes," I say. "A bunch of people do."

I imagine that she has leaped to the conclusion that Zeke and I share a back bedroom with a single bed.

"Maud says you took her underwear," she says, as though Zeke has reminded her of intimate subjects.

I am astonished that Maud could have the presence of mind to spend the afternoon having an abortion and then come home and check out her underwear drawer. She's a woman of steel.

"Four pairs," I say. "She has enough to outfit all Washington."

"Her favorites," my mother says.

"I'll return them."

"Do you eat regular meals?" my mother asks.

"I'll be doing the cooking," I say.

Zeke is coming toward the car, and I can tell my mother does not want to meet him.

"I don't like this arrangement at all," my mother says to me. But I have hopped out of the car and can pretend not to have heard her.

"Good-bye," I call gaily, knowing that she is too well brought up to make a scene in front of a half-naked boy in a yellow wig. She drives off without saying good-bye.

"That," Zeke says, pointing to the peak of the porch roof directly outside my bedroom, "is Albert Page."

I look up.

"Albert, this is Sophette," Zeke says.

Albert Page is sitting on the end of the peaked roof, straddling the peak like a pony.

"Hello," he calls.

"He could fall," I say to Zeke.

"What a terrific idea," Zeke says, and takes off his blond wig, setting it on my head. "Good luck. Have a first-rate afternoon."

10
The Unexpected Arrival of Homesickness

Zeke disappears, leaving the twins on the front porch and Albert on the roof.

"Zeke dead," Cassie says happily. She follows me in the front door with Thomas. The Reverend Page's casket has been moved to the hall and is closed. Thomas lifts the lid carefully and peers inside.

"Daddy gone," he says with great wonder. I look inside. There's a half-empty package of Salem menthols and a worn copy of a book called *On Death and Dying* on the pillow.

I walk up the steps and the twins scramble up on their hands and knees behind me.

My plan is to go to my bedroom and settle the

twins with the things in my backpack to entertain them while I climb out on the roof and persuade Albert to come in the house so his mother doesn't return to find him splattered on the sidewalk.

I find, when I get to my room, that Albert has taken the time to crayon I HATE YOU in red letters on the wall; to turn over the kitty litter box, spreading Litter Plus all over the rug; and to tear off my bedspread. The one-eared cat is sleeping on my backpack. Outside, on the roof, Albert has turned around—his back precariously close to the edge of the roof—and is watching me.

I decide to ignore him. First I will have to clean the kitty litter off the rug, or the twins will eat it while I'm on the roof rescuing Albert. I run downstairs to get a carpet sweeper and am away just long enough for Thomas to have one mouthful of kitty litter and for Cassie to be half out the window to the roof. I take my own washcloth and scrub I HATE YOU off the wall, leaving only a faint pink reminder of Albert's message to me.

"I DO HATE YOU," Albert shouts from the roof, watching me. I continue to ignore him.

"Albert bites," Thomas tells me as I clear the last bit of litter from his gum.

"I have no doubt," I say.

I remove the one-eared cat, settle the twins on the floor with my backpack, and begin to climb out on the roof when I hear a voice that I recognize immediately as that of the Reverend Page shouting from the sidewalk, "ALBERT PAGE. Go in off the roof right away."

Very slowly Albert makes his way across the peak of the roof and climbs in the window. I am sitting on the bed now, trying to ignore him but conscious that if I ignore him too much, he might bite, so I have a corner-eye view of him as he inches across the room, bops Thomas on the head with his fist, and races down the hall to his own room to which he shuts the door.

"Albert bites," Thomas says matter-of-factly, brushing his few front teeth with my toothbrush.

I hear the footsteps of the Reverend Page on the back steps, along the hall, past Albert's room. He walks into my bedroom, surprising me with the authority of his presence in full religious dress.

I am still sitting on my bed.

"We don't allow the children to play on the roof," he says.

"Albert was on the roof when I came back from my exam. He had spilled the kitty litter box and written that." I point to the I HATE YOU on the wall.

"Albert bites," Thomas says with a toothbrush in his mouth.

I am astonished at my boldness. I am also pleased to see how easily the Reverend Page has wilted under my attack. He sits down at the end of my bed, looking less like a man of God than he did—more like a skinny man in a black dress.

"Albert is a problem," he confesses. I am suddenly afraid he is going to cry right there in my bedroom with me and the twins in the room.

"He was born at a difficult time in our marriage."

"I'm sorry," I say. I don't know what else to say. It seems to me that they are still at a difficult time of their marriage, and I don't want to know about it. I can tell the Reverend Page is the sort of man who believes honesty between people comes from confessing the most intimate details of their private lives.

I am afraid he will go on and on, and that pretty soon I'll know why he sleeps alone in a casket and will hear about his friendship with the woman priest who got him fired—and so on. I read *True Romance* as a child and can imagine anything.

"That's okay," I say. "You don't need to tell me anything." I jump off the bed and pick up Cassie. "I can handle Albert."

The Reverend Page shakes his head sadly. "Maybe," he says.

I watch him go to the door of Albert's room, open it, and duck the small plastic truck that whizzes by his head and lands just at the door to my room.

"He needs a lot of love," the Reverend Page says to me before he goes back downstairs.

I take Thomas's hand and go down the back stairs. We go out in the backyard where there is an old rusted jungle gym that must have belonged to a family before the Pages. All afternoon I swing the twins and seesaw them up and down, up and down, and catch them at the end of the slide and hold my hand at their backs as they go up the slide—over and over and over again. I think the afternoon will never end, that I will never be in bed with a book, any book, even *U.S. History Since the Civil War*. Dr. Sally Page is two hours late. The Reverend Page is at a special service with the lady minister. He left me a note on the refrigerator that I saw when I went in to get juice for the twins. I have not had a chance to get staples and I have completely forgotten Albert until I turn around and he is sitting on the bottom back steps with a teddy bear whose furry paw is in Albert's mouth.

Albert is a beautiful child with square-cut blond hair and large wide-set eyes and a fine-boned face just in the process of losing its baby fat. He looks like an angel. No one who did not know him would believe me if I told them about his biting.

"Hello," I say to him.

He doesn't reply. He doesn't take the teddy bear paw out of his mouth but he is following my moves exactly with his eyes.

I stop swinging the twins and set them down in the garden.

"Swing, swing," they cry.

"More," Cassie shouts, lying on her back and kicking.

"More now," they say.

"No," I say. "No more."

Tomorrow, I promise myself, I will teach them to play independently, not to eat kitty litter, and not to cry when they want something. I am beginning to question why anyone would want a child. I wonder if we were like this as children. Certainly not me. Perhaps not Eliot either, but I can imagine, without much difficulty, Maud squeaking "More, more, more, more, more."

"Do you happen to know where my mother is?" Albert asks from the steps in a bassoon voice that knocks me dead. It is the first time I have heard him speak except for "I do hate you" on the roof.

"She went to a seminar," I reply. "She should be back by now."

"She's always late," Albert says. "Always."

"I'm sorry," I say genuinely.

"It's not your fault," he says.

I am beginning to have different dreams for the summer, in which scenes like this one prevail, with the twins screaming and Albert and me sparring in the backyard. I wonder whether I will ever lie in the hammock on the front porch and discuss God with the Reverend Page and the existence of love with Dr. Sally Page. Or whether I want to.

I was sent away to camp in Vermont when I was ten because my mother had to have a hysterectomy. She didn't tell me then or now what kind of operation she had, just that she was going to have it and that I would be much happier off in a lovely setting with friends my own age.

Well, she was wrong, of course. I went by airplane to Keene, New Hampshire, and got locked in the bathroom. I was in the bathroom when the plane landed, so the stewardess shouted at me. By the time I met the bus to Camp Newowana parked outside the terminal, I was feeling terrible. The bus was full of girls who seemed to have known each other since birth, girls with whom Maud would have had a lot in common, who stopped talking when I got on the bus and watched me walk, as though I were a sideshow attraction, to the back of the bus where there was one remaining seat next to a very small girl who appeared to have leprosy.

"MARY LEARY," the bus driver shouted back at me, and the busful of girls giggled at the comic possibilities of my name.

"Yes," I whispered.

"From D.C.?"

"Yes."

"Okay. We're off."

"I have a great-aunt in D.C.," the girl with leprosy said. "She lives in the Home for Incurables. Do you know where that is?"

As it happened, I did know where the Home for Incurables was. It gave me the creeps, and I didn't want to talk about it as the one common link we had in Washington, D.C.

"No," I said. "I don't."

Camp Newowana was a lovely setting for wild boar but at first glance, I doubted that, as a human child with no experience outside of a Georgetown row house, I would survive intact.

There were ten tents on platforms surrounding a lake that remained the temperature of ice water throughout the summer. There was a main lodge where meals were served, and we had to eat everything on our plate. I do not, as I have indicated, object to eating—except under military command. There was a large low building called Paradise, where there were fourteen toilets in cubicles, fourteen sinks, and fourteen stall showers. The final blow of my camp experience took place in Paradise my first night away from home.

I was lying in bed in my tent, which consisted of eight best friends from Westchester County in New York, the girl with leprosy, and me, and I had to go to the bathroom like anything. The counselor, Miss Pettin, to whom I had taken an immediate dislike because of the fact she disdained anyone who was not Olympic material, told me to get out of my bunk and pee before I wet the bed and froze. The eight best friends laughed uproariously.

I took my flashlight, put on my slippers and bathrobe, and made my way, across the high roots of pine trees jutting out of the ground, to Paradise. I expected boar and bear and foxes and coyotes to be lurking behind the trees, but every time I ran to escape a wild animal in pursuit, I tripped over a root and fell. By the time I got to Paradise, my pajamas were wet. But I went into a cubicle, sat down, and began to read the graffiti on the door. ALICE LOVES LARRY. ALF + LPT = LOVE. SARA LOVES MARGIE. HAHAHA. I KNOW WHAT SHE IS. MARY LEARY STINKS. I stopped and read again. MARY LEARY STINKS in bright blue Magic Marker and underneath in different-colored pens was written: AGREED. AGREED. AGREED. Three times. Maybe by three different people. Maybe all by the first. Who cares?

I felt a powerful surge of sickness come over me like stomach flu, and I thought I would fall over in the cubicle and die. I didn't cry, but I stayed there for the longest time, overcome by what I now understand to be homesickness of the worst kind, the kind that would not quit. Miss Pettin had to come after me.

"Constipated?" she asked, swinging open the bathroom door. "It always happens at the beginning of camp. There'll be prunes for breakfast."

"I thought I was going to throw up," I said.

"Oh, wonderful," she said. "Just what I need the first night."

I followed her back to the cabin. The homesickness lasted through the first week and off and on in powerful doses afterward. I never told my mother. I wrote her notes about the lovely setting and what a fine time I was having and asked how she was feeling after her operation. But when I came home in August, fifteen pounds thinner and the color of chalk, she asked me if I'd really had such a fine time.

"Well, I was a little homesick from time to time," I admitted.

I feel it coming now with Albert on the back step hating me and the twins screaming and Dr. Sally Page calling from the kitchen window had I had a chance to get the staples.

And I have chosen to run away from a house less than half a mile away, so homesickness must be a condition of absence more complicated than simply being away from home.

11
Albert Bites

"I didn't have a chance to get the staples," I say to Sally Page, carrying the twins up the back steps, trying to avoid stepping on Albert, who will not move.

"That's okay," she says.

I can tell she's in an irritable-trying-to-be-pleasant humor. "I guess we'll have hot dogs," she says, taking a package out of the freezer, "and beans."

"I'm sorry. I should have had dinner ready."

"I'm sorry I was so late."

"Oh, that's okay. Everyone was fine. Really great. We had a good day," I say—not, as you know, my usual manner of speech.

She smiles at me, knowing, I can tell, that I'm not telling the truth.

"I suppose Billy is out with Ruth at a meeting," she says.

It's the first time I've heard the name of the un-Reverend woman minister.

"That's where he said he was going."

"If it wasn't for his casket in the living room, he'd forget where he lived," she says. "Shit. No milk." She shuts the refrigerator door.

"I'll get some," I say, ecstatic for the chance to get out.

"And some fruit," she says. "And staples."

At this point I certainly can't ask about the staples.

"Is Albert upset with me?" she asks quietly, almost sadly.

"I guess he was, because you were late."

"Poor Albert." She shakes her head. "He didn't bother you, did he?"

"Nope." I was going to add that he hadn't had a chance to bite me yet, but I could tell it wasn't a good time for that kind of humor.

I make sure I still have the blank check Sally Page gave me, and I head up Newark Street to the Giant.

My mother goes to the market once a day or else she calls Neam's, and they deliver groceries in boxes on the front porch. I have never been sent for anything more complicated than a carton of milk or a loaf of thin-sliced diet bread. Never staples. I imagine, if I knew what they were, that we have staples on the shelves of the cupboard, but in all probability Harry at Neam's just includes them in my mother's order and charges her double, which, according to my father, is Neam's fiscal policy.

I arrive at the Giant at five forty-five along with the rest of the working public of northwest Washington, hot-tempered after a day put in for the federal government, banging their silver carts down the produce aisles, careless of the backs of bare heels and toes in sandals. I take a cart, park between two women at the peach bin, and fill a plastic bag with a dozen hard peaches at eighty-nine cents a pound.

"None is ripe," the woman on one side of me says.

"Put them in the window," the woman on the other side says.

"I want them tonight," the woman says crossly, as though those of us around her should take the collective responsibility for hard peaches.

I move on to plums, pleased to see a bite-size woman in a lavender lace dress, a flat straw hat, and a triple strand of yellow pearls. She smells too sweetly of G. C. Murphy's one-dollar-and-eighty-nine-cents-an-ounce perfume. I am pleased to see her because she is taking her time, testing plum after plum, so I am certain she will be happy to take the time to tell me about staples. I can tell she is a woman with nothing but time on her hands.

"There's salt, honey, and flour," she says. "You can have regular white or cake flour, double-rising, whole wheat, rye. They have rye here in two-pound, five-pound, and ten-pound bags—large as you could possibly carry. And sugar. Coffee—drip grind, or regular. Tea, if you take tea. My sister calls rice and noodles 'staples.' And chocolate. I always have a chocolate malt before I go to bed."

She would have gone on for the rest of the night, I am sure, if the woman who objected to the texture of peaches had not asked if we could move from the plums and take our talk elsewhere. I'm glad for the chance to thank the older woman, who has put one fat plum in a plastic bag and has moved on.

I decide on white flour and sugar in five-pound bags, a five-pound can of Maxwell House coffee, and orange pekoe tea. I get a bunch of bananas and a gallon of whole milk and buy *People* magazine with Lady Diana and Prince Charles on the front. My father won't allow *People* in the house. My mother says the magazine reflects the same human condition that leads people to have abortions. You guessed it.

"I love people," my mother says, which, I should mention, is a gross overstatement, "and *People* magazine makes a mockery of them. Even the Pope was spread on the inside pages when he was shot in the Vatican."

When I get back, Dr. Sally Page is sitting at the kitchen table with the twins and Albert.

"I'm sorry, we went on with dinner without you," she says. "The twins were cranky and hungry."

"I'm sorry. I should have had dinner ready," I say for the nineteenth time.

"It's been a hard first day for you, Mary," she says sweetly, and smiles at me with such a look of sadness that I forgive her lateness and disorganization and think again for the first time today that I'm glad I've left home and moved in with Dr. Sally Page.

As if to confirm my thoughts Zeke walks in the back door in gray-painted blue jeans and sits down next to his sister.

"Hello, Sophette, my beauty," he says to me, opening his mouth for Cassie to give him a bite of squished beans. "Is this all for dinner?" he asks Sally. "I had hot dogs for breakfast and lunch."

"The cupboard is bare."

"Bad day, Sal?"

She nods.

"Where's Jesus the Second?" he asks, stuffing a hard peach and plum in his back pocket from the groceries I'm unpacking.

"He is Risen."

"And out with the martyred Reverend Ruth?"

"What do you think?"

"I think, poor Sally," Zeke says, "divorce him."

"Not in front of Albert, Zeke."

"Then do it in private."

"You *know* what I mean. He has enough troubles."

"Jesus the Second or Albert?"

"Albert."

"Jesus is nice," Cassie says.

"Very," Zeke agrees.

"Jesus is dead," Albert says, mixing Nestlé's chocolate in his milk.

I wish my mother could be here at this moment to participate in this high-minded religious discussion. It would confirm her darkest imaginings.

Zeke takes down a bag of potato chips, takes two beers from the refrigerator, and tells me good-bye.

"Where're you going?" Sally asks, washing the catsup off Thomas's hands. "Out with Persephone?"

My heart sinks to my feet.

"You're lucky I'm not bringing her here," Zeke says to Sally.

"There's a Death Group meeting tonight. Why don't you invite her to that?"

"For the Reverend Page?"

They both laugh.

"Who's Persephone?" I ask.

"Goddess of spring."

"I mean Zeke's Persephone."

"She's at least forty and twice divorced," Sally says. "Zeke likes experience."

Well, I think to myself, that certainly deals me out.

"I'll read to Albert," Sally says, handing me Thomas. "And you put the twins to bed. I want to be out of here before Billy arrives with his group."

"You mean, you're leaving?" Zeke asks.

"I mean I'm going to bed."

The twins go to bed early with bottles, and I go downstairs and put away the rest of the groceries and wash the dishes. People are beginning to arrive. The Reverend Page comes into the kitchen with the un-Reverend Ruth, who is a slender mannish woman with short black hair and a boy's lilting walk. She looks, at first glance, like the kind of woman who would have gotten along swell with Miss Pettin at Camp Newowana.

He introduces me as a member of the family, although he can't remember my last name. He suggests that now we are both—referring to the un-Reverend Ruth and me—related, due to living in the house.

Upstairs, where I retreat as soon as possible, Sally Page is sitting on my bed. She looks much older than when I first saw her, and I wonder whether these changes have been recent or whether she has a remarkable capacity for putting up a good front.

"I'm sorry to throw so much at you today," she says to me, "but I want you to take over as much as you can of the children and the household duties this summer. I have an especially hard work project planned, and, as you can see, Billy is otherwise involved and not of much help."

I don't ask her how he is involved—whether she is referring to Death Group meetings or Ruth—because, in fact, I don't want to know.

I know enough for one day anyway and fall asleep immediately, not bothering to remove the one-eared cat from the pillow under my head.

I am awakened by Albert. I am actually awakened by a terrible pain in my hand and sit up in bed to find Albert standing next to me in pajamas. He has, I discover very quickly, just bitten my thumb. My immediate response is to bite him back and throw him out the window.

But instead, I ask him in a voice that surprises me with its reason, "Why do you hate me?"

"Because you don't like me," he says simply.

"I don't know you," I say. "I don't like or dislike you."

"Pretty soon you'll dislike me."

I move over in the bed and pat the empty space I've left.

"Get in," I say. I don't know why I do this instead of biting him back. Some instinct makes me gentle.

Albert hesitates.

"I bit you," he says, confused.

"I know," I say. I look at my hand with four small toothmarks on the thumb. "See."

"Does it hurt?"

"Sure, it hurts," I say.

"Then why do you want me to climb in bed with you?"

"I don't know."

That's an honest response, and Albert climbs in, pulls the covers up, and puts his head down next to the one-eared cat.

"Do you like Ifan?" he asks.

"I don't like cats," I say.

I move the cat to the bottom of the bed and lie down on the pillow next to Albert.

"Are you going to live here forever?" he asks.

"For the summer," I say. I don't add, "If I can stand it."

"Will you go on summer vacation with us?"

"Where do you go?"

"Block Island. To my grandmother's."

"Maybe," I say. "Your mother hasn't asked me."

"Maybe she doesn't know if we're going," he says. "She could be getting a divorce instead."

"Is that true?" I ask.

"I think it's true," he says. He moves his body closer until our bodies are touching and his hard skull is next to mine on the pillow.

In time I put my arms around him and watch him fall asleep.

I feel magical as I watch his quiet breathing, his soft sweet face near mine, as though I have tamed him.

And to my great surprise, I also feel a rush of warmth for my mother, who must have lain like this in my bed with me, though I only remember it like a shadow in my mind.

I want to call her to tell her. But if I were to do it, I would find the line busy. Because, in spite of my unexpected warm feelings for her, my mother is presently sitting at our kitchen table plotting the quick and absolute destruction of Dr. Sally Page's career.

Instead, I fall asleep with Albert next to me and wake up the next morning early to his small voice in my ear whispering, "I'm very sorry that I bit you last night."

12.
News from the Home Front

There is an envelope with my name on it lying on the kitchen table when I come downstairs at twenty minutes after seven.

"This was on the front steps when I got the paper," Sally Page says absently, feeding the twins. "Maybe it was left last night."

I open it. Inside there is a check made out to me from Maud Leary for two hundred dollars and a note that reads:

> Dear Mary,
> Thanks a lot. This was a terrific help.
>
> Love,
> M.

There are three hearts by her name that she has gone to the trouble to color in with yellow, red, and green Magic Marker. Don't ask me why I am touched by the gesture of three handmade hearts from Wonder of Wonders. I have definite weaknesses, such as this one, that are going to make it difficult for me to get on in the world. I put the note and the check in my wallet.

"Do you know what happens when you have an abortion?" I ask Sally Page nonchalantly. I wonder hopefully if I might strike her as the type who would be in a position to consider it.

"Not much," Sally says, washing Cassie's cereal bowl. "Particularly if it's early. Why?"

I shrug. I learned very early with my mother to avoid answering personal questions.

"Can it be dangerous?"

"Not often. When abortions were illegal, they were dangerous because they were performed by untrained people." She sits down with Thomas in her lap.

"Do they hurt?"

"Afterward. Sometimes I guess they hurt a lot."

I am certain she thinks I'm pregnant. I can see her looking at my stomach while I put away the Rice Krispies and granola. Maybe she'll tell Zeke. That ought to spark his interest in me. At least he won't think I'm a virgin any longer. Virgins probably bore him.

"Have you ever had an abortion?" I ask boldly.

She hesitates. It's my guess that the only reason she tells me is to warm up our confessional friendship so I'll tell her I'm pregnant.

"Yes," she says. "After the twins."

"And it hurt?"

"A little. But I had no choice. I knew I couldn't handle any more children."

"Was it easy?"

"Very. Nothing to it."

"Did you feel depressed?" I ask.

"Of course," she says, and thank God, just as she begins to tear up, Zeke walks in with green paint from the shutters in his hair and says that raccoons are in the garage and have knocked three gallons of green paint off the shelf.

"I'm at the end of my rope," Sally says. "Don't tell me about raccoons."

"You are always at the end of your rope lately, Sal."

"It's true," she says, washing the cereal off Thomas's face.

"Maybe you should turn celibate. Cut down the risks," Zeke says.

"I have already," she says, putting Thomas down.

"I'll clean the paint up," I say, glad for an opportunity to leave the kitchen.

"I hate martyrs," Zeke says.

"I'm not a martyr," I say. "I *want* to clean the paint, for chrissake."

"That's worse," Zeke says. "Anyone who'd choose to clean up paint must be demented."

"Right. That's the problem," I say, and leave the kitchen for the garage. "Are the raccoons still there?" I ask casually enough but, as you know, I don't even like domesticated animals.

"Yeah," Zeke says. "Rolling in the green paint. When you finish cleaning the floor, you might give the six of them a bath."

There are no raccoons in the garage and only one can of forest-green enamel-base paint has spilled but that, I discover as I am cleaning the floor, is plenty.

Celibacy must be a new condition for Sally Page, I think to myself. I wonder if the decision came as a result of the Death Group meetings or as a result of her abortion.

I wonder if Maud Leary is going to make a complete turnaround and become celibate. I wonder if she wept afterward. I can't imagine Maud weeping without a large audience. But then I can't imagine an abortion either.

On few matters do I agree with the mother of our Wonderful Family except on that one.

I remember a summer morning two years ago, just after Maud graduated from National Cathedral and before she went to Nantucket with Senator and Mrs. Nims and their lovely children for a family holiday of sun and fun. Maud was making me particularly sick at the time. She had lost weight so her stomach wouldn't fold over the new black bikini with a top the size of a small string. She had cut her hair, and miraculously it had curled at its new length so her face looked, I'm sure to even an ordinary passerby, soft and sensuous. And Mother had bought her two pairs of short shorts and skinny tops for her trip to Nantucket.

"You're encouraging trouble," I said, bad-tempered.

"What kind of trouble," my mother replied innocently. "Maud needs beach clothes, Mary."

"So do I."

"You're not going to the beach."

"What you mean is, my legs would look awful in short shorts," I said.

"You look better in trousers," she said with, I'll have to admit, perfect honesty.

"Anyway, I can just tell there's going to be trouble," I said, storming out of the kitchen with a handful of Fritos.

"This is a chaperoned vacation," my mother said crossly.

I shut myself in my room and sprayed so much perfume in my hair that I was almost asphyxiated. It took my mother exactly thirteen minutes to establish a plan to appease me and reunite our Wonderful Family in communal bliss.

I heard her bang up the stairs, march down the hall, and knock politely at my bedroom door.

"Mary," she called in. "Maud and I thought it

would be nice to go out to lunch. Just us girls."

"Yuk," I replied.

There was silence.

"It would mean a lot to me," my mother said.

I prefer my mother's steamroller approach to her poor-little-me approach any day. But the fact is, I was sunk. Anytime she uses the poor-little-me, I'm sunk—guilty, in other words.

"We're going to leave in half an hour for the American Cafe," she said meekly.

She knew she had me.

"Why don't you wear your nice little strawberry sundress," she said.

My nice little strawberry sundress made me look very much like an unharvested field of strawberry plants, flat and shapeless.

"I'll go," I said. "But I'm wearing overalls."

I looked at myself in the mirror. It occurred to me that if I didn't compare myself to Wonder of Wonders, I wasn't bad-looking. At the last minute before we left I decided to cut my hair with a nail scissors on the off chance that it would fall in curls around my face. Soft and sensuous. It was, as I said, an off chance.

"Oh, Mary," my mother said when I banged down the front steps in my overalls and mongrel haircut. "Why don't you like yourself better?"

Maud was sitting on the hall bench in a periwinkle-blue sundress with spaghetti straps and what must have been a recent silicone treatment, because her breasts were the size of cantaloupes.

"I *love* myself," I said dramatically. "It's the rest of the world I have some question about."

At lunch my mother ordered wine for her and Maud and a double chocolate malt for me because I insisted. Maud spoke pleasantly about her trip as though it were going to be an excursion of virginal bliss and her choice of courses for college and had the usual grace to ask Mother how things were going with Life Chance.

I ordered a jumbo hot pastrami and cheesecake for dessert and didn't talk.

When Maud got up to go to the ladies'—to redo her mascara, I presume, stopping on the way to speak to thirty-six of her best friends also having lunch at the American Cafe—Mother reached over and took my wrist.

"This should be the best time in our lives, Mary. You children are launched and we should be enjoying each other."

"Well," I said. "Things never are what they should be."

"That's not true if you believe in God and follow the Church."

"You believe in God, Mother, and things aren't as they should be for you," I said.

"Sometimes they are," she said.

"Bullshit," I said. It was not a nice thing to say and hurt her feelings, and I ended up, as usual, feeling awful and apologizing.

But I remember thinking then, exactly as I am thinking now, that just when things ought to be right, when you've worked very hard to make them so, something happens to overturn the applecart.

I finish cleaning the green paint and wash my hands in turpentine and then the hose. I think of my mother and Life Chance. There she was, preaching against birth control to us and, lo and behold, she's got worse than birth control to deal with. And it's her own doing. I feel terrible for her. If she knows about Maud's abortion, which is possible, then she's probably half sick, wandering around the house in her buttoned-up white blouse and navy blue skirt, waiting for a three o'clock appointment with the priest. She is thinking what a failure she has been as a mother. I don't want children, I decide. It's altogether too chancy.

I wipe my hands on my overalls and am about to go inside when Zeke comes to the door to say my mother's on the phone.

ESP. She is the only person I know in the world who really has it.

"Mary," she says when I take the phone. "Something is the matter with Maud."

There you have it.

I sit down.

"What?" I ask.

"I don't know. Something serious. She won't eat and she won't come downstairs. Please talk to her."

"I can't if she won't leave her room," I say.

"Call her. Just hang up now and call back, and I'll go get her."

I do just that.

Mother answers as though she is surprised to hear from me.

"Mary, hello," she says loudly with enthusiasm.

"Can I speak with Maud," I ask.

"Of course," she says. She ought to have been an actress in musical comedy.

"Maud," she calls. "Maudie, Mary's on the phone for you."

There is a very long silence in which either Maud has refused to answer or recommended that Mother tell me to drop dead.

"It didn't work," my mother whispers into the telephone.

"Is she sick or upset?" I ask, fearing the worse.

"Both," my mother says. "I think she's had a fight with Jonathan."

Honest to God, my mother is so innocent, she would never make it in musical comedy in spite of her talents. She ought to have been a nun.

"Yeah, probably," I say, knowing it's likely that a botched abortion and subsequent depression have sent Maud to her room.

"Why don't you call again after lunch," my mother says. "I'm going to be making some calls now."

"Sure," I agree. "I'll try."

It is my guess that she's planning to call the priest to come over and talk Maud out of her depression. But, as usual, I'm wrong.

13.
The Virgin Mary and Other Martyrs

I have never thought of my mother in general as quick to act. She is deliberate by nature and likes lists of all kinds, arrangements, and Serious Discussions to precede any action. Unless, of course, she is hurt.

Hurt, my mother moves like a cat—sure-footed, circling her prey with an instinct to kill, pouncing at exactly the appropriate moment. She never misses the jugular, if that's what she's after.

When Eliot was hit in the head with a brick thrown by Alvin Starkey, my mother was at Mrs. Starkey's that afternoon with a hospital bill for Eliot's stitches. Mother also added that if Alvin did not first go to Confession and then apologize to Eliot in the presence of Eliot's father, she would speak to Father O'Lanigan, our priest, herself. So she said darkly to Mrs. Starkey. And Alvin did.

When Tracey Lingrin teased me in the locker room about my belly rolls, calling me Jelly Rolls, my mother, to my horror, called Sister Grace, who called Tracey Lingrin to Mother Superior, and Tracey was suspended for un-Christian conduct.

And when Mrs. Spencer Holt, widow of a former Secretary of War, who lives next door to us and busies herself by peering in our windows, said to Mother that it was none of her business, but if Maud didn't protect herself, Mother might be a grandmother before she was forty-five, Mother sued for defamation of character. Of course, the suit didn't go any further than a letter written to Mrs. Holt on my father's legal stationery, but we put up a high wooden fence between our gardens, and Mother didn't plan on speaking to Mrs. Spencer Holt again.

And I've already told you about her stand on what's good for children and what isn't—as in nihilistic books or Dr. Sally Page.

So I should not have been surprised that it took her less than twenty-four hours from the time she let me out at Sally Page's on Newark Street to arrange for Dr. Page to be brought into the office of the Academic Dean at Georgetown University in the first step toward her dismissal as an assistant professor of sociology without tenure.

According to Zeke, if she'd had tenure, they

couldn't have fired her unless she bombed the university or slept with the president's wife. But since she had another two years to go before her name came up for tenure, it certainly wasn't in her favor that my mother presented an ironclad case against her as a feminist pro-abortionist in a Roman Catholic school—albeit Jesuit, and therefore liberal—still answerable finally to the Pope Himself, or himself, as the case may be.

Eliot told me some of the details of the story later. It went like this:

When Mother came home from dropping me off at the Pages', Eliot was in the kitchen studying, with minor interest, for his Greek Literature exam. So he was able to catch most of what went on—and able as well to describe for me the look on the mother of our Wonderful Family's face when she came into the kitchen with a set jaw and white lips and called Aunt Ethel. With Aunt Ethel she discussed her game plan. In fact, according to Eliot, Aunt Ethel was quite helpful, and Mother, to my great surprise, spent a great deal of the conversation listening.

The plan, worked out in the kitchen while Eliot was pretending to be absorbed in *The Odyssey,* was this:

Mother called for an appointment with the Academic Dean for the next morning. She said to him on the telephone that she was Professor Leary of the law school's wife and that she had a child at

Georgetown—namely, Wonder of Wonders, hardly a child—and therefore had a Great Interest in the university; and that the delicate and urgent matter she wanted to discuss with the Dean had to do with a certain untenured assistant professor—no names mentioned—who was flagrantly undermining the principles of Christianity—of Catholicism, in particular—and, I suppose, Judaism, Buddhism, et cetera, et cetera, as well.

The following morning, according to Eliot, Mother went to Mass and Confession and was back making breakfast at seven-thirty so he wouldn't be late for his Ancient History exam.

That afternoon, when Eliot came home with Pauline to smoke dope and watch the soaps in the basement, Mother was reporting the day's events on the telephone to Aunt Ethel. She had worn her wraparound skirt, a white blouse, my grandmother's gold cross, stockings, and black stack heels. Honest to God. She went through all the details of the outfit to Aunt Ethel—leaving out the underwear, according to Eliot—and I believe him. She had talked to the Dean about Sally Page's moral disintegration as evidenced by her husband's being fired. She had somehow, champion sleuth that she was, discovered he was not fired because he inducted the un-Reverend Ruth at all, but for other reasons, which I'll get to later. She had described to the Academic Dean the talk Sally Page had given at Georgetown, other conversations she had heard

Sally Page have with students—invented, of course —and had topped it off by describing Dr. Page's abduction of her daughter as though Sally Page were the Reverend Moon in the form of a woman. So there you have it. The Academic Dean called the President, the President called the Chairman of the Sociology Department, and Mother gathered her one hundred and eighty pounds, tucked neatly into her black skirt and white blouse, and headed home, Victor of the Meet, a gold medalist from God.

Eliot had the extraordinary good sense to look up Dr. Sally Page's number in the telephone book and call me, finding me at three o'clock in the afternoon knee-deep in squashed carrots thrown on the kitchen floor by the twins, who were presently being entertained, to my complete disgust, by the one-eared cat giving birth to three wet and bloody kittens in a box in the middle of the kitchen floor.

"Listen, it's Eliot," he says when I answer.

"Hi, Eliot," I say, expecting the worst, expecting for a moment that Mother has jumped from the roof onto the statue of St. Michael, leaving a note to my father that reads: "Because of Mary."

"I thought I'd better call you," Eliot says. "Because I've been sort of hanging around the kitchen lately, listening to Mother and Aunt Ethel, and I get the idea that Mother's trying to have that woman where you're living now fired from her job."

"You're kidding," I say, pulling the kitten box over beside me, so Thomas, who is looking wild-eyed, won't pick up a kitten and squeeze it to death.

"That's how it sounds. Mother went to George-town today and told the Dean that Sally Page is a pro-abortionist and so forth. You know Mother when she gets going. She could run for President, and she's mad because you've left home."

"Jesus," I say.

"Yeah, well, I thought you'd want to know."

We talk some more but it is obvious that Eliot is aching to get to the beginning of *The Edge of Night.* So we get off and I pick up the twins, move the kitten box to the corner of the kitchen, and go out to the backyard.

Zeke is on a stepladder painting the trim on the third floor. Albert is next door biting someone, and I don't have the energy to swing the twins or read to them or play with them in the sandbox or even to read the new John Irving I found among the Pages' cookbooks.

I sit down on the back steps and am still there when Sally Page comes home, walks down the back steps, kisses the twins absently, sits down on the patio across from me, and says I'll have to leave.

"Leave?" I say, stricken, not expecting this kind of trouble. "I just came."

"Leave," she says, and I can tell before she starts that she is going to cry. "Your mother, whom I don't think I've ever met, is trying to get me fired."

So there it is. The holder of the blue ribbon, God of our fathers' own servant in time of trouble, is over the finish line for another victory.

I feel the adrenaline necessary for warfare leap in my blood.

"I won't leave," I say to Sally Page.

14
Initial Failures

Of course, my first idea for revenge has to do with
Maud.

It is my guess that either an infection has set in
from the botched abortion, or else she's having a
delayed reaction to sinful acts in the form of acute
blues. Maybe she, too, will run away from home, so
I'd better establish plans before she has the opportunity.

The fact is, like all good Catholics, my mother
has a list of sins and punishments that have a
hierarchical order. It's my guess that abortion
comes second or third, preceded by disobedience
to parents and maybe atheism. Someone like Maud
Gonne, who's had an abortion, is in far greater
need of absolution than Sally Page, who has just

recommended it as an alternative—I mean, my mother doesn't need to know she's had one. Innocence is bliss.

This will be my approach, carried out by telephone:

"Hello, Mother. This is Mary. I understand you have plans to force the resignation of Doctor Page."

Pause.

"I hear from a reliable source."

I think of red-eyed Eliot, head-to-foot with Pauline in front of the soaps, and decide not to reveal my source.

My mother will not shirk at my attack.

"OF COURSE," she thunders. "As a representative of a Jesuit school, she advocated abortion to young Catholic women in a public forum. It is my duty."

"'Judge not, lest ye be judged,'" I say. Her words.

"For what?" she says.

"How is Maud?" I ask cunningly.

"The same," she replies.

"Well," I say, "you ought to ask her whether minor surgery is responsible for her present state of mind."

"What?" my mother asks, understanding my implication immediately. "How do you know?"

I will hang up without replying and sit on the kitchen stool at the Pages', imagining the ensuing scenes.

Like an elephant attacked by wasps, my mother will charge upstairs to Maud's room. Maud will be lying on her back, tears pouring down her face. When the mother of our Wonderful Family lumbers into the room, she will put a pillow over her face.

"I *know* what has happened," my mother will say. It is clear, and always has been, that the best defense is a good offense.

"How?" Maud will ask weakly.

"A reliable source," my mother says.

"No one knows," Maud says.

"Evidence," my mother says.

"Did you call the doctor?"

"Stand up and let me take a look at you," my mother says.

Maud stands up dutifully and, in doing so, the brand-new diaphragm in its beige plastic case purchased for the future, falls out of the pink flowered pillowcase where she has hidden it.

"Oh, Maud," my mother says, collapsing on a chair, weeping buckets. "That too?"

It's a swell scene, and I come out a winner, since with this scenario, Mother—given the deep troubles in her own backyard—forgets all about Sally Page. However, it's not at all the scene that takes place, as you probably have already guessed.

"Hello, Mother," I say. "I'm calling back to see how Maud is." My voice sounds heavy with dark suggestion.

There is a pause.

"Maud?"

"You told me she was in awful shape when you called this morning," I say.

"I'd almost forgotten, Mary. She's absolutely fine now. She came downstairs right after we talked and had a bacon, lettuce, and tomato sandwich and went to Lord and Taylor to look for clothes to take to France."

There is a beep on the line, which means that another call is coming in for my mother. She puts me on hold and is gone for four minutes by the clock on the stove.

"Mary." She comes back breathless and excited, as if the Pope is on the other line calling from the Vatican with news of her premature sainthood. "This is a Very Important call," she says. "I'll talk to you later."

And that's that. It doesn't take extrasensory perception to guess that the Very Important call has to do with Dr. Sally Page, and any chance I had to use Maud Gonne is down the drain.

15.
Revenge,
Et Cetera

"Tell me about your mother," Sally Page says to me.

We are sitting at the kitchen table, eating a dinner of overdone pork chops, sticky mashed potatoes, and a salad with lettuce leaves the size of rowboats. I have made dinner. Sally Page isn't eating.

"I'm sorry," she says. "It's not the dinner, which is lovely. I just can't."

She is limp and folded, like a thin cotton dress with the starch washed out. I hardly recognize her as the same woman I met at Georgetown University. The twins are playing with pots and pans on the floor. I have put the box of new kittens in the broom closet on the off chance that they can survive the twins. And Albert—poor Albert has been sent home from the next-door neighbors for pushing and shoving, et cetera, et cetera. The list was long. He has pulled his chair next to mine and is leaning against me, putting a kind of personal pressure on my shoulder as though he would like to become permanently attached.

"My mother is a steamroller," I say. "That's why I left home. I was going to be flattened into the dining room rug."

Zeke comes in the back door and sits down.

"A shitty deal," he says to her, kissing the ends of her fingers. He does not kiss the ends of my fingers.

So he knows. She has told him in the garden while I was in the kitchen overcooking the pork chops. So much for my plans with Zeke on the back stairs.

"What do you think will happen?" he asks.

She shakes her shoulders, and I can tell she is going to cry again. "I didn't do anything," she says. "Nothing at all. I gave a reasonable talk. I had no idea you had really run away from home," she says to me.

"Mama cry," Thomas says.

"Mama is fine," she says to Thomas.

"Death Chance is what they ought to call your mother's organization," she says, and goes up the back stairs. We sit in the kitchen and listen to the door to her bedroom slam shut.

"Life Chance," I explain to Zeke. "My mother is head of Life Chance for Washington. They're against contraception for Catholics," I say, letting Albert climb on my lap and press his head into my chest.

"Very enlightened," Zeke says to me. He sits down and puts his feet up on the kitchen table. "I haven't seen Sally cry before."

"I'm sorry," I say.

"I think you should leave," he says. "You're a good kid, but I honestly think you should go."

"I can't," I say, getting up and clearing the table.

"What's keeping you?"

"I don't want to leave," I say. "I know I can help out here."

"It's been a real circus so far."

"This morning you liked me, I could tell. This morning you thought we'd get along fine."

"Things change," he says, picking up Thomas and Cassie and starting up the back stairs.

"I'm not my mother, you know," I say.

"Fact is, Sophette, my little kitten, before we had you, we didn't have your mother. Life here in the Center for Thanatopsis wasn't paradise, but it was okay. We got along."

"I'm really sorry," I say.

"It's not your fault," Albert says, helping me rinse the dishes.

"Yeah. It is, sort of," I say. "Bad things seem to happen when I'm around."

"Me too," he says with sympathy.

I take down the box of kittens, since the twins

are gone, and sit with Albert on the floor, watching them. The one-eared mother has licked them dry, and their thin coat of fur is fluffed, their eyes closed, their bodies stretched out against their mother's belly. They are sucking like mad.

I have a strong instinct to rescue. When I was small, my favorite reading was along the lines of Robin Hood and King Arthur. I am attracted to people in trouble. When I think about my virtues— which I try not to do, since I can never come up with a large number of them—I always count rescuing as one.

For example, I get along best with my mother when she thinks, as she does every six months or so, that she's having a nervous breakdown. I tell her to lie down on the chaise, and I bring her plenty of food and tell her about the good parts of my life, even if I have to lie.

I am known at school as a friend to the underdog—like Jaya Dorcas, who has a harelip and no friends, two things that may or may not be related. As far as school is concerned, there's no salvation to being a friend to the underdog, because there shouldn't be, in a fine competitive Christian school, any underdogs—only winners and achievers—which just goes to show the understanding an institution has for the nature of man and his limitations. But I have no choice. I was born to rescue, and whatever doubts I had about life at the Reverend and Dr. Page's fly out the window this minute as I suit up to pull Sally Page from the ferocious jaws of the mother of our Wonderful Family.

Maud answers the telephone when I call. She speaks in her pure Vermont Maple Syrup voice, so I imagine she was expecting Jonathan.

"Hello," I say, not bothering to introduce myself by name, although if I hadn't stolen her best bikini underwear, she would have forgotten me by now.

"You flunked History," she says thoughtfully. "The notice came today."

"Any other good news?" I ask.

"Just that you've really *hurt* everyone by leaving, Mary."

"You sound broken in two," I say. "I called to speak to Mother."

"She's not here."

I know Mother is there. She is always there unless it's four and she's at the market, or before breakfast and she's at Mass, or occasionally late afternoon and she's picking up Eliot at St. Alban's. But Wonder of Wonders insists she's not there.

"Do you want to speak to Daddy?" she asks coyly.

Maud has a killing sense of humor. If there is anyone in the world I do not want to speak to when I've flunked History and run away from home, it's my father. I can feel his disappointment in me the twenty-three blocks between my house and the

Pages migrating like black locusts through the hot June air.

"That's okay," I say. "When will Mother be back? I really want to speak to her."

"As a matter of fact, Mother is on her way over to see you." I don't know why Maud doesn't choke on the artificial sugar in her voice, but she doesn't, and wishes me well, a good summer, et cetera, et cetera. She doesn't even add about the underwear I stole just to let me know that she's an honest-to-God turn-the-other-cheek Christian.

I hang up.

"My mother is coming here," I say to Zeke, who has come downstairs after putting the twins to bed.

"What a treat," he says.

"My mother never goes out at night. She never goes anyplace."

"Maybe she'll be kidnapped on the way."

Albert comes downstairs carrying *The Wind in the Willows,* and I promise to read to him on the front porch while we swing in the hammock.

I construct a scene for my mother's arrival: I am lying in the hammock with Albert under my arm, reading *The Wind in the Willows,* a cat on my stomach; Zeke is in the rocking chair, his feet on the rope of the hammock, swinging it gently. A scene of domestic tranquillity.

Just then the doorbell rings, Albert runs to the front hall, and by the time I arrive from the kitchen, my mother has stepped inside and is standing next to the Reverend Billy Page's casket, which is open.

To my great surprise I am not sick in the middle of the hall.

"This is Albert Page," I say, dumbstruck by my own ability to pull myself together. "Albert, this is my mother."

My mother shakes his hand.

"This is my father's casket," Albert says, earnestly catching my mother's eye on the open casket.

"I'm sorry," my mother says, full of the rehearsed sympathy of one familiar with funerals.

"It's all right," Albert says, obviously confused. "He only sleeps there."

I explain quickly and without success about the Death Group.

My mother is holding a Lord & Taylor package and a large bottle of red liquid the color of summer cherries.

"I brought you these," she says, handing me the packages. "Aunt Ethel brought this over to you today," she says of the red liquid. "Your cousin Terry drinks it for breakfast and lunch and has lost fourteen pounds. But she eats a regular dinner, even mashed potatoes and dessert if she wants it." She hands me the other package. "I'm going on a diet too. Maybe by the end of the summer, when you come home, we'll both be thin."

My mother has never gone on a diet before. In fact, she has never provided me with an incentive like Aunt Ethel's red diet-juice to go on one—saying instead, "You must lose weight," while she fills me up to the top with macaroons and chocolate chip cookies.

I open the package and can see, nested in tissue paper, three pairs of bikini underwear—one with beige lace and lavender flowers, one pale yellow, and one black.

"Do you want Maud's back?" I ask too quickly. "Is that why you got them?"

"I got them because I wanted to," my mother says simply. "I didn't come for Maud's."

"The Pages' basset ate her purple ones anyway," I say, not knowing what else to say, touched and embarrassed as well by this strange offering of friendship in the form of diet drink and bikini underwear. I can tell she is uncomfortable, too, and says she must be off to pick up some library books for Eliot. She tells Albert good-bye and says she hopes I will call from time to time—by which she means every day—and leaves, tripping over a blond-striped cat on the porch.

I think of my mother as cumbersome but in control, not awkward. Seeing her now, in a house with caskets for living men, full of cats and dogs and misplaced toys and broken furniture with dirty fingermarks and food on the woodwork, I understand why she leaves the careful order of our house only when it's absolutely necessary. She cannot adjust. This knowledge about my mother touches me as well.

I have not, however, forgotten that in spite of her sudden kindness to me she has spent the day arranging to have Sally Page fired. So I follow her to the car.

"Thank you for the bikinis and stuff," I say. I am in the process of planning a quick attack that begins, "I don't understand how you can, on the one hand"—this is the language of my father, useful to lawyers—"get Sally Page fired and then, on the other hand, act as though a Wonderful Family is the most important value in the world!" but before I have a chance to order my thoughts, she has grabbed my wrist, given me a huge air-blocking hug, and said, "I'm afraid these people will turn you into a child I'll never recognize as my own."

"I'm not yours," I say. "I'm my own."

She gets in the front seat, behind the wheel.

"Why are you trying to get Sally Page fired, Mother?"

She starts the engine. I have never known my mother to walk away from a Serious Discussion in my life, and I want to detain her.

"She supports the whole family. Her husband lies in his casket all day. If you get her fired, these children will starve to death."

"Children don't starve to death in America," my

mother says, and she is crying. My mother simply doesn't cry—ever. In fact, according to a story told me by Maud during one of the very rare occasions when she and Mother were fighting, Mother's tear ducts were surgically removed when she married my father, at his request.

"Children starve in America all the time," I say. "In the ghetto. If you ever got outside your air-conditioned Catholic world, you'd see them ten blocks from our house—with distended bellies and maggots in their hair." I have a tendency to over-dramatize, as you know, but I have never—and you must believe me—spoken this way to my mother.

"Don't be extreme," my mother says softly.

"Thank you for the bikinis and stuff," I call after she has pulled away. I don't need bad dreams full of guilt.

I read Albert two chapters of *The Wind in the Willows,* and he falls asleep in my arms. I carry him upstairs and put him to bed in his clothes. Sally Page's door is open. The light is off, but I can see that she is lying in bed, fully clothed, with her arm across her forehead, and Zeke is sitting in an armchair in her bedroom.

I go downstairs, turn off the lights, and sit in the hammock on the front porch.

Zeke opens the screen door and sits down on a wicker rocker, rocking back and forth so the only sound we hear above the din of cars on Connecticut

Avenue is the squeak of the rope hammock and the monotonous beating of the wooden rocker on the wooden porch floor.

"I'm sorry," I say.

"Don't be such a Catholic," he says. "It doesn't help."

"I'll leave," I say.

At first he doesn't answer. I consider saying it again with an edge, more dramatically perhaps, but wisely, I wait.

"Don't leave now," he says. "I've changed my mind. Albert seems to trust you, and he's never trusted anyone in his life."

"Me neither," I say.

I swing back and forth. He rocks back and forth against the background of a black and soundless house. I am thinking about him kissing me.

He will get up, stand for a moment in the darkness, and then lean down and kiss my lips for a long time. I pretend he is kissing me now. I don't even hear him when he whispers my name from the other side of the porch, because I am imagining him beside me.

"Shhh," I hear him say. He has stopped rocking.

"Look," he says.

I stop my hammock and look in the direction Zeke is looking, beyond the streetlights, into a blackness that gradually takes on the form of the Reverend Billy Page leaning down toward someone else obscured by his head. I guess from Zeke's expression rather than my own critical eye that they are kissing.

They stop, part, and walk up Newark Street about fifty yards to the house and up the path to the front porch.

As they reach the top step of the porch Zeke says in the deepest voice I have ever heard, but not loud, "Discreet, aren't you?"

The Reverend Billy Page starts.

"You surprised me," he says. "I didn't see you."

Zeke doesn't say anything.

"Did anyone call?" he asks, recovering. "I've been at a clergy meeting and met Ruth there. Zeke?"

"I don't answer phones," Zeke says.

"Is that a moral position?" the Reverend Page asks coolly.

I know it is my turn.

"No one called," I say quickly. "I was here all day."

"I'm glad of that," the Reverend Page says. "We're turning in now. Is Sally here?"

"In a manner of speaking."

"Where?"

"In bed."

The Reverend Page and Ruth go inside. From the kitchen we can hear they are having an argument. Then the kitchen light goes off. Zeke gets up and closes the front door.

"I'd like to string him up by his feet in the bell

tower of the cathedral," Zeke says to me. "Aren't you glad you moved into this terrific family?" He leans over the hammock and kisses me—not on the lips, as I've been imagining, and not long either. About one sixteenth of a second at most. But he does kiss my forehead, and for a long time I can still feel the place like a burn where his hand touched my shoulder.

16
St. Michael Bites the Dust

So the cat is out of the bag.

At least I know what's up at the Pages' house on Newark Street—and certainly Zeke does and Sally Page in the bedroom across the hall from me does. I suppose the Reverend Page climbs into his casket every night and closes his eyes, pretending to concentrate on death and the afterlife. Lo and behold, as soon as the house is quiet, he hops up the back stairs, where the un-Reverend Ruth is praying for the ordination of women. No wonder he sleeps until noon.

I try to imagine my own father in the place of the Reverend Billy Page. But I can only think of him in a beige suit at his desk or in the classroom at Georgetown University or in the backyard next to the statue of St. Michael, reading the editorial page. It is difficult to see him having a polite conversation with another woman, unless it's his secretary.

If I were to tell my mother about the lives in this house, she would fly to Confession to be cleansed of overheard sins.

I have left the door to my bedroom open. I haven't even put on a nightgown and am sleeping on top of the bedspread in case a need develops for a quick getaway. I am considering dramatic circumstances. Zeke running after the Reverend Billy Page with a shotgun. The un-Reverend Ruth setting fire to the house and jumping to safety. I have a sense of impending doom. At least life in the bosom of my Wonderful Family had a certain safety.

Sally Page is out of bed now and has gone to the bathroom to wash her face. She leaves the door open, so I can see her examining her eyes in the mirror. I am surprised to see her head toward my room and wonder, too late, whether I should jump under the covers and appear to be asleep.

"Mary?" She is standing in the doorway. "Are you awake?"

It is obvious that I am awake since she catches me in the process of leaping, fully clothed, under my covers.

"Yup," I say, and turn on the light. She tells me to turn it off. We can talk in the dark. I know it's because she doesn't want me to see that she's been

crying. She sits down at the end of my bed. In a
nightgown, with her hair down, she looks frail—
not at all the kind of woman who would send her
students to abortion clinics as a matter of fur-
thering their education.

"Zeke says you know about Billy."

What can I say? I shake my head yes because I
am too dumbfounded to risk speech.

"I don't know what to do about it."

She's asking *me* what to do—the very girl who
wanted to go to public school to lose her virginity
and who remains, at sixteen, lily-pure, untouched
by human hands. I have enough trouble deciding
what to wear.

"Zeke tells me that you and Albert get along."

"Yes, we do," I say.

"Poor Albert has had the worse time. You know,
he bites. It just started when things got so bad
between Billy and me."

"I know. He bit me."

She puts her head in her hands and rests it
against her knee.

"Not hard," I insist. "Only a little."

"He bit the next-door neighbor very hard. I had
a call from the neighbors to say he can't come over
again."

"He told me he pushed the boy next door."

"Bit and pushed. They are calling a social
worker."

This is too much for me. I am thinking about

my cozy bed next to Maud Gonne's bedroom and wishing I were in it.

"Of course, Albert's upset. Who wouldn't be, in this family?" she says. She takes my hand, which I have put on my stomach. "I'd like you to stay until things are straightened out here," she says. "I'll pay you more, of course."

I do not bother to ask what I'll be paid with after my mother gets her fired. It seems, at the moment, a question beyond the point.

"That's okay. Don't worry about the pay. I'll stay for the summer," I say bravely.

"What are we going to do about your mother?"

"Beats me," I say.

"Can you do something to stop her?"

"I'll think of something," I say.

She leans over and kisses me on the forehead.

"You are an angel," she says.

As you can well imagine, no one has ever called me an angel before. Sally Page has me hooked. I wouldn't leave her now if there were civil war. I lie in bed thinking of my angelic qualities and wake up in the morning fully clothed and with a plan about my mother.

It is a plan learned from spending sixteen years as the younger sister of Maud Gonne—one, in fact, that she could have designed herself although, of course, in her hands it would have been executed with grace and would not have failed because of the fatal flaw I did not foresee. The problem is that the plan is based on a kind of deception and false sweetness with which I am unfamiliar. The concentration it takes for me to be insincere prevents my anticipating a turn of events.

So this is the plan: I take the twins and Albert on a bus down Wisconsin Avenue to R Street and walk down R Street to my house. By the time I get there, it's ten-thirty: Mother is talking on the phone to Aunt Ethel, Eliot is working at Swenson's, Maud is sleeping late, and the twins are bad-tempered from the long walk. I am very pleasant to everyone—my mother, the children—even Maud, who wanders down in her nightgown for coffee. My mother is impressed by my patience with the children and overwhelmed—it's my hopeful guess—by feelings of maternal love. I do not play my cards too soon. I let her play with the twins and watch her give Albert juice and cookies. I apologize profusely for failing U.S. History and am willing to engage in a Serious Discussion about our Wonderful Family without complaint. At the appropriate moment, when one of the twins is cuddling in her lap, I say very gently, "Mother, you certainly can't carry through with your plans for Sally Page."

Here I am, after all, as compliant as Maud Gonne, a model daughter, returning like a lamb to the fold.

"Certainly not," my mother says, and calls the Academic Dean while I am sitting there.

"Drop any complaints I've made about Doctor Sally Page, please," my mother tells the Dean. "I was altogether wrong."

So there you have the plan which, as you will soon see—in spite of its excellent design—does not work out.

I take the twins and Albert on the bus down Wisconsin Avenue to Georgetown.

I hold Cassie on my lap and give Thomas to Albert to hold on his lap.

"NO, NO, NO," Thomas screams at the top of his voice so everyone in the bus fixes his eyes on me. "Albert bites."

"No," I say to Thomas.

"NO, NO, NO," Thomas shouts. So I bring Thomas on my lap with Cassie.

"I hate Thomas," Albert says.

"Shhh," I say to Albert. I wonder if I look old enough to be their mother, I am thinking, when Albert decides he will not sit next to Thomas on the bus.

"Sit down," the bus driver says.

"No," Albert says.

"ALBERT BITES," Thomas shouts.

"Excuse me," the lady in front of us says to me, "but will you please have your little girl stop taking the hairpins out of my hair."

I have not noticed that Cassie has been quietly taking the hairpins from the bun of the lady in front of us and putting them in her mouth.

"Give me the hairpins," I whisper.

She shakes her head.

I can see three or four hairpins sticking out of her lips, and I pull them. Cassie takes the last one out of her mouth and throws it across the aisle.

"There," I say pleasantly to the woman in front of me, handing her the hairpins. "I'm so sorry." I should tell you that the one thing I learned in Catholic schools was to say 'I'm so sorry' with great feeling. Very occasionally, like today, it doesn't work.

"I certainly wouldn't put them in my hair after they have been in that child's mouth."

I consider saying she's made a wise decision, because the child is just recovering from rabies, when Albert bops Thomas on the head. I decide to get off at T Street and walk the rest of the way.

Somehow, as I scramble out of my seat, Cassie has managed to hook her little fingers in the woman's pinless bun and pulls it apart completely.

"I am so sorry," I say to the woman, to the woman next to her, to the bus driver.

"They are not mine," I want to shout as I disembark.

"I'll never have children," I say to Albert as we are walking along Wisconsin Avenue.

"What'll you have, then?" he asks me thoughtfully.

"Nothing at all," I say. "Just myself."

"That's not very much to have," he says, not unkindly—and I would have to agree with him.

My mother is not on the telephone with Aunt Ethel. She is sitting in the living room in a red wrap-around skirt with appliquéd umbrellas on the front —suitable for someone nineteen—a white shirt with appliquéd umbrellas on it, and red flats. She is not alone. The twenty-one-member board of the Washington Chapter of Life Chance is sitting in the living room with her.

The problem with knowing what is going on in the living room before you go in the house is that Mother keeps the drapes shut so people on the street will not be able to look in at our Wonderful Family gathered in blissful harmony around the fireplace.

So it is not until I am in the front door with all the children, and Thomas has run into the living room on his short fat legs, announcing, "Daddy dead," to the Life Chance board, that I realize that my plan as designed doesn't have a chance in hell of working.

Thomas, of course, is accustomed to large gatherings of people in the living rooms of houses, and although his general experience has to do with people in caskets, he is not at all put off by twenty-one women sitting in chairs with china coffee cups in their laps.

"Daddy dead," he says again with the distinct pleasure of an audience.

I pick Thomas up.

"Excuse me," I mumble to the group of women. "I came to visit. I'm sorry to interrupt."

My mother, unabashed, introduces me to the Life Chancers—to each one of them in turn, Honest to God, as if this is a social trial. By the time we are halfway around the circle and I am extending my hand to Mrs. Everett Aiken while Mother explains that Thomas's daddy is not really dead, only practicing, there is an incredible crash in the back of the house.

I've probably been in the living room going through these introductions for a total of five minutes. I have Thomas in my arms, and Cassie is sitting on the floor emptying the contents of Mrs. Everett Aiken's purse on the Oriental rug. Albert, I assume, is hanging back in the hall, sensibly not wishing to be introduced to the board of Life Chance.

I am wrong, of course.

Albert must have left the hall immediately, gone to the kitchen, which has a large glass door opening onto a deck that overlooks the garden and the statue of St. Michael.

I do not know what it was about the statue of St. Michael that drew Albert to him. I do know that Albert went out the back door, across the deck, down the steps, and climbed up St. Michael, who is, as it turns out, less formidable than he seems.

According to Albert, St. Michael rocked back and forth, and, as Albert scrambled to get down, St. Michael fell over and lost his head, the fingers of his left hand, and his right foot. Albert, who somehow fell away from the statue, skinned his elbow and both knees.

By the time Mother and I get to the door, the head of St. Michael is still rolling across the slate patio and Albert is sitting on the ground inspecting his wounds.

My mother takes us home then by car and the twins fall asleep on my lap.

"I'm sorry about Saint Michael," I say to my mother.

"I'm sorry," Albert says quietly to her.

"Mary," she calls, after we are all out of the car and Zeke, who is on the front porch when we arrive, has taken the twins upstairs for a nap.

"Yes," I say, looking into the car window.

"That little boy has severe emotional difficulties," she says.

I know without asking that my plan has failed. Mother, fired with enthusiasm, pulls away from the curb. Not only is Sally Page unfit to teach. She is unfit to mother as well.

17
AWOL
Again

"Trouble," Zeke says as I walk up the front steps. He is leaning against a white pillar in his painting clothes and drinking a Molson.

"Bad trouble?" Albert asks.

"Yeah," Zeke says. He hands me the beer. "Have some."

I don't normally drink, but I take two swallows of beer in a gesture of conspiracy. Albert drinks the rest and throws the can in the trash.

"He's been drinking since he was two," Zeke says to me as I follow him around the back of the house, down the driveway, and through the back gate. "It's Billy's idea that he won't be an alcoholic if he learns to drink early. Maybe Billy thinks he won't die if he practices dying early."

Zeke opens the screen door and I follow him into the kitchen. "Be quiet," he says. "Your sweet papa has company, Albert." Albert and I follow him up the back stairs. The twins are in their beds calling, "No nap, no nap." Zeke gives them their blankets and shuts the door. Now they don't just cry—they scream exactly as though we are beating them to smithereens with billy clubs, and they have only minutes left on earth.

Zeke walks across the hall into my bedroom and falls on the bed on his back. "Shit," he says. "I suppose the visitors downstairs are going to think we practice Japanese torture on babies for kicks." His arm is thrown across his eyes, so I can't see much of his face, but already I have guessed that he's in a terrible mood. Albert sits down next to his legs and I sit on the floor next to the kitty litter box.

"So what's the trouble?" I ask.

"I broke a statue at Mary's house is one trouble," Albert says.

"It was no big deal, Albert," I say.

"Yes, it was," Albert says. "Your mother was so mad, she almost popped."

"Wonderful," Zeke mutters under his breath.

"It wasn't wonderful at all," Albert says. "I *hate* trouble."

"Well, lemme tell you, Albert," Zeke says, pulling himself up and leaning against a pillow, "for a guy who hates trouble, you're in plenty of it."

The visitors gathered downstairs include Mrs.

Applebaum from next door; Mr. Applebaum, her husband; Mrs. Applebaum, Senior, her husband's mother; and Dr. Wyatt Dickson, a psychiatric social worker. The Reverend Billy Page is sitting on a hardback velvet love seat with his feet on his casket, smoking Turkish cigarettes with the first two fingers of his right hand. He is very glad to see Zeke and me as we come downstairs without Albert and jumps up to introduce us to the Applebaums. He calls me Mary Perry—Perry happens to be Zeke's last name—either because he has forgotten mine or else he wants us all to seem related.

"The Applebaums," he says, "have come about Albert. They have brought Doctor Dickson with them because he is an expert on children." In fact, as I soon find out, Dr. Dickson is the shrink for Philip Applebaum, age six and a half, and former best friend of Albert.

The psychiatric social worker has come along to explain the damage to Philip's sensibilities as a result of Albert's biting, et cetera, et cetera.

"You know, of course, that he bites," Mrs. Applebaum says, as though Albert is in the habit of swallowing people like Philip Applebaum whole in a single gulp.

Zeke and I are sitting on the couch across from the Reverend Billy Page and directly to the side of Mr. and Mrs. and Mrs. Applebaum and the shrink. I see Billy Page nod in solemn agreement, and I follow suit.

Not Zeke.

Had I known Zeke was going to blow his cool, I never would have nodded in agreement with the Reverend Billy Page.

Zeke slaps his hands on his thighs, sits straight up, and looks at the Applebaum contingent as though they are in the process of turning into a lower form of animal life before his eyes.

"If I didn't have a serious case of hoof-and-mouth disease, I'd bite you all," he says.

He doesn't need to leave in such a hurry as he does. The Applebaums have developed a sudden need to get home. They shake hands quickly with the Reverend Billy Page—all but the shrink, who slinks quickly and ratlike out the front door, believing, I imagine, that, hoof-and-mouth disease notwithstanding, Zeke might fly back into the hall and bite him on the thigh.

That scene of heroism has done it for me. I am hopelessly in love. I float airborne into the kitchen, where Zeke is sitting on the counter eating a peach.

"You were wonderful," I say.

"You," he says in a voice as cold as dry ice, "were a shit."

In my room with the door shut, I think of extreme measures:

Jumping headfirst from the roof:

156

My darling Zeke,
I did this because of you.

Leaving on a plane for Australia:

Zeke darling,
I have to go halfway around the world to get away from you.

Going home:

Dear Zeke,
You have ruined my life. I have returned to my Wonderful Family, where I will rot and die.

I am lying on my bed, facedown, with my head in a pillow. It is completely dark in the pillow, and so, with my eyes open, I can imagine complete scenes—including my funeral, with Zeke kneeling beside my casket. In fact, that is the exact scene I am imagining when Zeke walks in, shuts the door behind him, and sits down on my bed.

"Albert's gone," he says.

"Gone?" I lift my head from the stage of my pillow.

"You heard correctly, Esmeralda. *Gone*," he says. "Disappeared."

18
New
Developments

I am to stay with the twins, Zeke says. He is going to look for Albert. It is clear to both of us that Albert escaped out the back door while we were sitting in the living room with the Applebaums. He probably listened at the top of the front stairs until he was sure the way was clear, then crept down the back stairs and bolted, over the back fence, dropping into the Applebaums' driveway, then up the driveway to Newark Street. He probably had almost an hour's head start, but my sense of time is fuzzy since I fell in love with Zeke earlier today.

Bolting, however, I understand. My heart goes out to Albert Page. I hope he bites my mother, his father, and Mr. Owens, who flunked me in U.S. History.

While the twins are sleeping I check his bedroom for signs of his departure. I can tell that he was reading *Charlotte's Web* for a while before he left because he's left it facedown on the floor and open to page 124, just before the death of Charlotte. He took his red backpack full of baseball cards and a picture of Jesus, from the neck up, given him by his father. If you have to have a picture of Jesus, this particular one is my favorite, and I'm sure you've seen it knocking around. In it he looks like a regular man who might have lived in a commune in California during the sixties. I have not gone into my feelings about religion with Albert yet.

It looks as though he might have taken his pajamas and the small panda that usually sits on his bed. The only surprising thing about his room is that he's taken off the bedspread and sheets and left them in a pile in the middle of the floor. I am remaking the bed with clean sheets when Cassie comes in and tells me she is going to spill.

"Spill what?" I ask, my back to her, not bothering to turn around until too late to realize that *spill* means 'to throw up,' which she has done on the thick tufted carpet in Albert's room.

I do not have time to give any more consideration to Albert's running away. I am down on my hands and knees, cleaning up the red carpet with a bath towel, which I plan to wash before Dr. Sally Page comes home from her incarceration, when Thomas begins to cry.

"Thomas spill," Cassie says hopefully. And she's right on target. I go into the twins' room, and there is Thomas, standing at the bars of his crib, looking down at the bright blue carpet.

"Thomas spill," he says without apology.

So it is with twins—a double dose of everything —and as I clean the bright blue carpet in Thomas's room, I fantasize about Maud marrying the son of the senator from North Dakota and having two sets of weak-stomached twins.

There is a number for Dr. Salinger in the kitchen.

"I am Mary Leary," I say to the doctor. "I take care of the Page twins, who have both just thrown up."

I know that my voice sounds as though I am calling from the middle of a nuclear disaster, but I can't help it. Nor can I answer any of the questions that he asks me. Do they have a temperature? Headache?

How do I know? They can't talk.

What did they eat? he asks me. Call him back, he says, when I have these answers. I take Cassie's temperature first. When I take it out after three minutes, timed on the alarm clock in my room, I cannot read the temperature.

"Shit," I say.

"Shit," Thomas says, happily playing with the new kittens.

"Kitty die," I say ominously.

"Kitty dead," he says, smiling.

I grab the box of kittens, check all the small ugly tabbies for signs of life, and shut them in Sally Page's room. Now Thomas is crying. In fact, Thomas is screaming at the top of his lungs, and I hear the heavy footsteps of the Reverend Billy Page on the front stairs. He bursts into my room.

"Please," he says to me. "You'll have to try to keep Thomas quiet. I'm having an important meeting downstairs."

If I had a choice of marrying the Reverend Billy Page or Azy, the male orangutan in the Washington Zoo, I'd choose Azy without hesitation. Dr. Sally Page must have been suffering from premature dementia when she met him.

I manage to keep my temper. "Can you read thermometers?" I ask over Thomas's screams.

He takes the thermometer and turns it around in his fingers.

"Normal," he says. "Perfectly normal."

He picks Thomas up. I should add that I have not changed Thomas's clothes since he spilled, so the Reverend Page's black cassock, which he is wearing this morning, has been ruined.

"Dammit," he says, dropping Thomas to the floor. "You might consider cleaning him," he says and marches off to the bathroom to wash his cassock.

I doubt if the Reverend Billy Page is one of

God's chosen prophets, if there is such a thing. My guess is, he chose himself.

I call Dr. Salinger with the news of the twins' temperature. He is busy, the nurse says. I wait while Cassie turns over the cat's milk on top of her head, while Thomas colors in red crayon on the linoleum floor, while the Reverend Page asks me to *please* get off the phone and keep the children *quiet* during his important meeting in the living room.

"I am talking to the doctor," I say. "Do you know that Albert has run away from home?" I ask with accusation.

"If I had a dollar for every time Albert has run away from home, I'd be a rich man," he says. He casts me a look that can only be described as un-Christian and leaves the kitchen.

Dr. Salinger is obviously bored with my report on the twins.

"Stomach virus," he says like a recording. "Clear liquids all day. Ginger ale, Seven-Up, apple juice. Plenty of rest."

This summer is beginning to look like the longest summer of my life. It is likely I'll be one hundred and ten by September—white-haired and bent-over double with arthritis—too old to retake U.S. History After the Civil War. On the calendar above the sink I see it is the fourth of June. I have only been working for three days, and already arteriosclerosis has set in.

162

While I clean the milk up off the floor and rinse Cassie's milky curls under the spigot, my mother, in the form of a saint, looms into view. I am beginning to understand that she was a woman of elephant strength to survive Maud and me and Eliot. No wonder she has thick legs, I think, and in the midst of this reverie about my mother, the telephone rings, and—to my absolute surprise—it is Maud Gonne on the other end of the line.

"Hello," she says in a frail voice that I hardly recognize. "How's everything?"

"Magnificent," I say boldly.

"I was sort of wondering if you were busy today," she says meekly. Meekly—I'm not kidding. The very Wonder of Wonders who parades like a Viking princess nude in front of our full-length mirror.

"I'm absolutely free," I say. "In fact, when you called, I was lying in a hammock under a willow tree, sipping lemonade and gin."

She is dumbfounded, I can tell. She doesn't say anything.

"I mean, I have time to talk," I say.

"Actually I'm at the People's Drug Store at Newark and Wisconsin and was just thinking of dropping by your place for a while, if it's okay."

"Sure," I say. I don't ask her what she's doing at the People's at Newark and Wisconsin, a block away, since there is a perfectly good People's at Q Street by our house. Already I suspect that it is not sisterly concern that has brought Maud Gonne to my doorstep but a Serious Problem, as my Mother would say.

And I'm right.

"The thing is, I want to talk to you about Jonathan," she says. "He's met somebody else he likes better."

Well, wonder of wonders. Jonathan Nims has dropped the beautiful Maud Leary for another broad. I suppose that'll teach her the dangers of lurking in recreation rooms. She ought to have had the baby and called it Jonathan Nims, boy or girl. She ought to have charged him, plus interest, for the abortion.

I grab both twins and run upstairs, feeling for Maud a mixture of sympathy—honestly—and elation, a mixture that is loaded heavily on the side of elation. In a flash I change the twins' beds, dump all the soiled clothes in the washer, put the twins down for a nap with bottles of ginger ale, so by the time Maud Gonne arrives at the Pages' house on Newark Street, I am, in fact, lying on a hammock sipping lemonade without the gin and reading, for lack of anything else immediately at hand, *On Death and Dying,* which I grabbed from the top of the Reverend Page's casket while he was otherwise occupied with his very important meeting in the living room.

19
Wonder of Wonders

Nothing short of the Stigmata could have prepared me for the vision of Maud Leary walking up the steps of the Pages' house. She looks older than God. She looks worse than I look in the morning before I take a shower, and she's wearing my blue jean overalls, which hang like a gunnysack around her hips. She looks like a red-eyed vision of Hell. Little does she know she's come to the right house —the only house with more caskets than furniture. I try to treat her arrival as ordinary.

"Hello," I say.

She flops on the other end of the hammock and bursts into tears. I'm not kidding.

"*Death and Dying*," she says, regarding the book

facedown on my stomach. "Exactly how I feel." This is spoken between sobs. "Dead and still dying."

"Jeez," I say, stalling for time, a little at a loss for words.

She gets right to the point.

"Jonathan met this girl at a party last week and fell in love with her—on the spot, according to him—after only one beer. Boom, he says—like that. He doesn't even want to *kiss* me any more."

Much less anything else, I presume, but I don't say it. In fact, after all the terrible things I've told you about Maud, I feel ashamed. Not that she hasn't been awful, just that I may have misjudged her, and in spite of my belief to the contrary, she does have a heart after all. Presently broken, but that just goes to show that she had one all the time—only she did one of the best camouflage jobs I've ever seen.

"Shit," I say to her by way of sympathetic comment on the whole situation.

"I'll say," she says.

"I couldn't tell Mom," she says. "She simply wouldn't understand at all. 'More flowers in the field where you found that one,' she would say. 'Other sheafs amongst the wheat.' 'Remember what I told you. Don't put all your eggs in one basket.'" She imitates perfectly our mother's predictable conversation.

"Not bad." I smile, secretly pleased to know that the angel of my mother's life has objections to her as well.

"And Daddy," she says. "He wouldn't say anything, but in his heart of hearts he'd be thinking, Too, too bad for Maud. She lost her hook on the senator's son and she may not have another chance for the big catch."

"What did you tell Jonathan?" I ask stupidly, since, as you well know, I haven't a clue how it would feel to be dropped inasmuch as no one has even bothered to pick me up.

" 'Bug off,' I said. 'Maybe she'll turn out to be a boy,' I said and then I threw his high school ring down the toilet in the recreation room and slammed my finger in the door as I left." She holds up a purple index finger on her right hand.

"Shit," I say.

"Is that all you can say?" she asks.

In fact, it is all I can think of. In our sixteen years as sisters, Maud has never confessed a single secret to me, unless you could call her general disgust at my existence a secret. I am astonished.

"I *hate* Eliot," Maud says. "After Jonathan dropped me off forever, I went down to the basement to tell Eliot, who was stoned and in the middle of watching *Search for Tomorrow*. 'If you don't mind, Maud, I want to see the rest of this show, and then I'll hear about your tragedy!' Can you believe it?"

I can believe it.

"Then I go upstairs and interrupt Mother, who's on the phone with Aunt Ethel about a Life Chance meeting, and say, 'Eliot's stoned, doped up, zapped.' I guess I must have screamed it, because she's been trying to have a Serious Discussion with me ever since. So I decide to come here. I wish I were pregnant."

"Well," I begin. To be quite frank, I'm at a loss for words. Every thought that comes to mind has the ring of 'I told you so,' and even I am a better human being than that.

"Well, what?" she says, putting her feet on the wooden brace of the hammock where I am lying.

"Well," I blurt out. "You were pregnant. Why didn't you stay that way?"

"What do you mean?" she asks, giving the impression, I promise you, of perfect innocence.

"You know," I say—a little confused, I'll have to admit. "When you got the two hundred dollars from me."

"Why did you think I was pregnant then?"

Jeez, I think to myself.

"Why else would you have needed two hundred dollars?"

"Mary," she says, sitting up, taking her feet down. "You thought I was having an abortion?"

"Well." I shrug. I'll have to admit, she's a hell of an actress. "It crossed my mind."

"Jonathan wanted a stereo and I got it for him with the two hundred dollars."

You could have knocked me over with a feather. I believe her. No one could make up a story like that and lie straight-faced and stupidly as she's doing.

"I was sure you were pregnant," I say, dumb-founded.

"I never did anything to get pregnant," she says.

"You didn't?"

"Nora Leary's daughter? Are you kidding?"

"What did you do, then?"

"Kissed. Kissed. Kissed. Kissed." She kicks over the rocking chair. "I should have gotten pregnant and had an abortion." She stands up next to the hammock and sticks a pillow from the chair under her shirt.

"I am so sorry, Mother, I did exactly what you told me to do and never used any contraception at all," she says. "Life Chancer's Daughter, Pregnant by Senator's Son, Has Abortion." She prances around the porch, holding her pillow.

"Mother would die," I say. I am, I should tell you, slightly horrified. I had never imagined this of Maud, as you know. So I'm glad to see Zeke traveling east on Newark at a pace, running toward the house. In the confusion I had almost forgotton about Albert.

"He's gone," Zeke says, collapsing on a wood and wicker chair. "I went to every house in the neighborhood, to the park, even to the school playground—everywhere. And he's gone. Call the police," he says. "And you have to call Sally."

I explain to Maud about Albert and his disappearance. I tell her about the statue of St. Michael and the next-door neighbors with the trained psychiatrist on a leash. And then I introduce her to Zeke when he comes out, after I try to call Sally and tell the Reverend Billy—certain that my fate with Zeke is sealed—that Zeke is, at this very moment, in spite of serious concern about Albert, falling in love with my sister.

"I know he's somewhere close," Zeke says. "What I'd do in Albert's shoes is hide close to home. Nowhere dangerous. I'd try to scare everyone except myself."

So the three of us look everywhere in the house and yard—in the basement, in the closets of the attic, and under the front porch and back porch where there's crawl space with room enough for a grown man. And no Albert.

"What about next door?" Maud asks.

"No." Zeke shakes his head. "Albert's already in hot water next door."

We look in the large azaleas and rhododendron bushes lining the side yard and in the garage behind the trash cans. Nothing.

"If you were running away, where would you go?" Zeke asks Maud.

"Until today I never thought of running away,"

Maud says. I'm getting ready for the sob story that will enlist Zeke's sympathy and set their romance in gear. But today Maud is full of surprises.

"I guess I'd go buy things. Bubble gum and comic books. Stuff I was never allowed to have."

"Where would you get the money?" Zeke asks.

"I'd steal it from my mother," Maud says without hesitation.

Wonder of wonders. I have certainly been off the track about Maud Leary. All these years she was probably involved in criminal activities while the only evil I imagined her capable of was my own personal favorite evil on the couch in the senator from North Dakota's basement.

Zeke goes into the house and calls the police and Sally Page, whom he cannot reach because she is meeting with the Dean about a serious matter and cannot be interrupted, Zeke says, shooting me a killing look.

"Well," I say. "I guess that's the end of my life on Newark Street."

"It's probably the end of Sally's life at Georgetown," Zeke says crossly.

"What's more important—Sally having a job or Albert being lost?"

"It's not a question of value but a question of fact. Both are true," Zeke says, looking up Newark Street for the police.

"Maybe not about Sally," I say, meekly acknowledging to myself that my love for Zeke is doomed by his failure to return it.

"Fat chance," he says. "So what would you do if you ran away, Sophette?"

"If I were Albert, I think I'd go to my mother's house and see about fixing the statue of Saint Michael."

That comes off the top of my head. It has never crossed my mind until this very second as I watch a patrol car pull up and two matching fat policemen hop out.

"Brilliant thinking, Marie Antoinette," Zeke says, going down the steps to meet the policemen.

But already I'm two jumps ahead of Zeke, the freak, wondering whether, in fact, Albert will be able to find my house again. After all it was only this morning that we were there and, in spite of tendencies to bite, Albert otherwise has a first-rate brain.

20
Two Peas
in a Pod

The Reverend Billy Page is not pleased to be interrupted by Zeke with two city policemen, but he does excuse himself from the meeting, leaving the un-Reverend Ruth in charge.

"Have you looked everywhere?" he asks Zeke.

"Everywhere," Zeke says.

"At the park?" the Reverend Page asks. "He often goes to the park."

The policemen follow Zeke and the Reverend Page onto the front porch. I go into the kitchen with Maud and look in the freezer for something to serve for dinner, selecting chicken.

"You cook?" Maud asks.

I nod.

"Jeez," she says, impressed. "Do you think he could have been kidnapped?" she asks.

"Nope," I say. "I think he's run away. I'm sure of it. He's like me, and that's what I did."

Maud is standing awkwardly in the Pages' kitchen. I have never seen Maud uncomfortable before, and it occurs to me, watching her stand in the middle of the Pages' house with ministers and caskets and young kittens inching across the kitchen floor, that she probably feels right now very much the way I have felt all of my life: out of place.

"Why did you leave?" Maud asks. I pour a glass of lemonade for both of us. When I get the ice tray out of the freezer, I find that Albert has frozen his collection of dead roaches in each one of the twelve squares.

I put the ice tray back in the freezer.

"Yuk," Maud says. "You're keeping those?"

"They're Albert's," I say matter-of-factly.

I am wondering whether I should tell her why I ran away—what she will do with this information and whether I should trust her with it. In the middle of my thoughts Maud says, "I used to think about running away because of you."

Well, you could have blown me over with a whistle.

"*Me?*" I say.

She shrugs. "Didn't you know that?"

"What in the world for?"

I am beginning to feel giddy, as though I'm in the middle of a long joke and have forgotten the punch line.

"Because Daddy liked you better. And Mother identified with you."

"Yeah," I say. "We're both fat and mediocre."

"I guess the real reason is that you've always said what you thought and done what you wanted to do. Like you're not even afraid to flunk U.S. History, for example."

"Sure," I say. "That was something I was dying to do. Flunk U.S. History so I could have another joyous year with Mr. Owens and the Great Depression."

"You know what I mean."

"I think you've developed premature senility," I say. I take down a package of Oreos. This conversation is making me hungry.

"You have always been pretty and smart," I say. "And I have always been fat and failing to live up to my potential." I take six Oreos and split them, one by one, licking the icing in the center.

"The way I see it is that I have been thinner than you but not as pretty and with less potential," Maud says.

It occurs to me that this could be a con game, that she wants her bikini underwear back, or else wants me to capture Jonathan and drop him and his girlfriend headfirst down the elevator shaft at the Hay Adams Hotel. That she wants to move into the top bedroom with Zeke for the rest of the summer and have me make them lemon swizzles for afternoon tea.

"Why haven't you ever told me this stuff before?" I ask.

"I suppose because I knew you didn't like me."

I buy that. It's a statement with a ring of truth, and I cannot help but admire Maud Gonne for saying it. Moreover, I can feel in my bones that I'm beginning to soften up when Zeke dashes in the kitchen to tell me to leave Maud with the twins, to look everyplace I can think of for Albert, and that he is off with the Reverend Billy and the police.

I will have to truthfully say that I'm glad for this opportunity to postpone my conversation with Maud.

"Do you mind staying with the twins?" I ask.

"I guess not," she says.

"You'll forget all about Jonathan after an hour with the twins," I say with assurance.

"I don't know if I can handle them. I've never baby-sat for little children before."

"Don't worry," I say. "You'll be fine."

And then to my astonishment I hug her like a giant mama bear. The hug comes out of nowhere. I just feel it coming on, as if my arms are being manipulated by strings.

The trouble with me, I think to myself as I dash down the front steps of the Newark Street house, is that I'm easily won. A real soft touch. A pushover with piano-stool legs.

The reason I know that Albert is at my mother's is that Albert and I are alike. It is as though we were hatched from the same pod of slightly irregularly shaped peas with extra-hard shells and squishy insides. I guess I knew that from the moment that Albert bit me on the hand and then crawled like a baby into my bed.

My thinking, if I were Albert, would go like this: I am very upset about St. Michael, and his breaking is a Sign of bad things to come. And then, to confirm my worst fears, there in the living room of my house when I come home after devastating St. Michael are Mr. and Mrs. Applebaum with a shrink who is talking to my father about *me*. I listen from the top of the stairs to the complaints and then very quietly I leave by the back stairs. It is absolutely clear to me that what I must do is go back to St. Michael's house and repair the damage in order to reverse the bad luck.

I reach the bus stop just as the D6 rumbles down Wisconsin Avenue. It is three o'clock by the clock at the bank, which changes to ninety-four degrees and then to June 4, while the bus picks up three summer school students at Cathedral School. They sit down in front of me and talk so I can't miss a word about a party at Henry Somebody's, where one of the three girls got drunk on rum punch and the other got kissed by Henry S. Which reminds me that I have probably lost Zeke forever.

I wonder if he's rushed back to the Pages' to kiss Maud, and what, if that's the case, he does with the two policemen and the Reverend Page while he's kissing her. By the time the bus reaches Reservoir Road, I have dismissed the love affair between Maud and Zeke on the grounds that it is impossible. Also, to my great surprise, on the grounds that I'm no longer—or at least not this afternoon—jealous of the lovely Maud Leary. The last girl on earth I'd want to be, in fact, is the one dropped by Jonathan Nims, the fart.

I get off at Reservoir and walk home. The front door to my house is open, the coffee cups and cake plates are still in the living room, where they were being used only this morning by the lead groupies in the Washington Life Chance movement, and Eliot is in the kitchen on his second quart of milk, getting ready for the late-afternoon TV shows.

"H'lo," I say.

"The prodigal daughter returns." He smiles, pleased with himself at this little joke.

"I'm just coming to pick up some clothes," I say.

"Maud's?" he asks.

"Yours," I say.

He laughs.

"Where's Mother?" I ask.

"Kneeling by the statue of St. Michael, praying for the forgiveness of your sins, you nerd. Where do you think she is?"

I go out the kitchen door onto the deck and there sits the mother of our Wonderful Family in a

178

lawn chair eating chocolate chip cookies like we used to do together during our Serious Discussions. And holding Albert Page on her lap.

So, you see, my instincts are unshakable.

21
The End of
the War

Occasionally in my life, I have had a revelation in
which I understand something I have not under-
stood before. Like what happened today when
Maud came over to the Pages. My mother would
say this Revelation is from God or the Virgin Mary,
depending, I suppose, on the nature of it, and I
should be eternally grateful for His Gift. My father
would say that it's not a Revelation at all but a step
in one's development toward maturity—ho-hum.

What is happening to me as I stand on the deck
watching my mother with Albert Page is more like
the Visit-from-God sort.

Boom. The Word in a cloud of smoke.

I understand my mother.

Suddenly I understand her Serious Discussions
and her pressure to make a Wonderful Family, her

chocolate chip cookies and macaroons, and her preoccupation with God and with the Virgin Mary. Even Life Chance.

I see her looking like me—a bit older, rocking babies and changing them, cleaning floors, burning dinners—but mostly I see myself, sitting on her lap as Albert.

I like her. She is a good woman—narrow-minded, of course—like anyone who is afraid of the confusions and changes in the world and has to protect her children from them. But she does honestly believe in the chance for life. And so do I.

"H'lo," I call down.

"How did you know I was here?" Albert asks.

"I guessed," I say.

"We've been having a Serious Discussion," my mother says, getting up and taking Albert by the hand.

"I bet," I say. "Everyone thought you ran away from home."

"I did," Albert said.

"They've called the police."

"No kidding," Albert says as he climbs up the back steps.

"Did Mary tell you that she ran away from home once?" my mother asks.

"Did you? When you were my age?"

"Recently," I say.

"This is my fourth time," Albert says. "It's the first time I've run away by bus."

"I better call Zeke and tell him I've found you."

"Where did you go when you ran away?" he asks.

"Your house," I say, dialing the phone.

"No kidding," he says.

Maud answers the telephone.

"I'VE FOUND ALBERT," I say, screaming into the telephone over the twins' cries. "I found him at our house. Is everything okay?"

"Really terrific. I've never had such a good time. You must be a masochist to work here."

"I am," I say. "I'll be coming right back with Albert."

"Maud's with the twins," I tell my mother.

"Maud?" my mother says, raising her eyebrows. "I have never imagined Maud with babies."

"Did you imagine me with them?"

She puts the lemonade in the icebox, the cookies back on the shelf.

"Yes," she says. "I've always thought that we are a lot alike."

I shrug.

"I suppose we are," I say.

When I leave with Albert, she is talking to Aunt Ethel about the coincidence of Albert running away. "Mary is really very capable and responsible," I hear her say as I walk out the front door.

Later that night, after the twins and Albert are in bed, I am sitting in the kitchen talking with Sally Page when my mother calls to talk to Sally. Not to my

182

surprise my mother does most of the talking, but I can tell by Sally's remarks why my mother has called.

"I understand," Sally says. ". . . Of course. . . . Don't worry about it. . . . The Dean told me today. . . . Thank you for calling," she says.

I know my mother has called the Dean and withdrawn her complaints.

"I bet she told you she's going to Mass *and* Confession tomorrow because she feels so bad," I say.

We both laugh.

"I'd like you to stay through the summer, Mary. I will need your help, and so will Albert," she says. "Billy is moving out."

"I thought he might be," I say.

"Well." She shrugs. "It'll be nice not to have a houseful of caskets. I'm afraid you arrived at our house just as everything was about to explode."

After Sally goes to bed, I go out on the porch. Zeke comes out while I am swinging on the hammock.

"So I guess you know what's up around here, Sophette."

"About the Reverend Page?"

"And your mother."

"Yup."

"Me too. Someone's got to paint the house."

He swings my hammock with his bare foot.

"I'm glad you're staying," he says.

Although he doesn't kiss me, I know that in the two months we have together in this house, he'll probably get around to it.

22
The End

I go upstairs to the small room where the cats and I live, turn on the light by my bed, and sit down. The night is hot, even for Washington in June, and exceptionally still. I can hear everything—the twins' soft breathing in the room across the hall, the quiet slap of Sally Page's bare feet across the bedroom floor as she gets ready for bed, Zeke doing sit-ups to WETA all-night music in the tiny attic room, and the cry of cats, probably the Pages', fighting in the alley behind the house.

I haven't even unpacked since I arrived three days ago so I do it now, putting away the nightgowns and trousers and bikini underwear stolen from poor Maud, who needs it now much more than I do. I am planning, of course, to stay for the summer and help Sally Page and make some extra money. Perhaps I'll buy knickers in the fall. Or a new dress.

In a package from Lord & Taylor are the bikini underwear my mother brought me and the red diet-drink from Aunt Ethel.

I try on the one with lavender flowers and look at myself in the full-length mirror, completely naked except for the bikinis. I am not, as you know, in the habit of doing this, since I don't like to spend whole days depressed. It was Maud who made an occupation of mirrors, back then—three days ago —when I thought she believed she was beautiful, loved by Jonathan Nims, and pregnant.

I know it will come as a shock to you, but I don't look bad. In fact, I look rather pretty in the face if I take off my glasses so you can see my face. And I'm not fat. Not slender, of course. Fleshy, I'd have to admit, but not fat.

I put on a nightgown, rearrange the cats on the bed so I can pull down the covers, and go downstairs to get *The Hotel New Hampshire,* which is still in the bookcase with the Pages' cookbooks.

It is ten o'clock, not too late yet to call Pamela Flower and tell her I've made a hundred-and-eighty-degree change since she saw me two days ago in the U.S. History exam. It is difficult to explain to anyone that you have changed unless you've lost twenty pounds and started wearing silver stars on your cheeks—besides, this change has only been visible to me for the past two hours so I shouldn't expect an astonishing response from Pamela Flower or Katie Aster, and I don't get one. I tell Pamela that yes, we'll go to Battery Kimble as usual this summer and talk about next year and invent troubles we have with boys.

When I hang up the telephone, I wonder about Eliot. Probably I have misjudged him too. He may be lying on the couch with Pauline's feet in his face, inventing mathematical formulas or thinking of nuclear disasters or considering the metaphoric implications of *The Odyssey*. It may be that his eyes are red from crying about romantic poetry. Nothing I used to be so sure about is certain. Even my father. He may simply be afraid to let me know what he feels, like I am. He may be the kind of man who works hard out of self-defense. I don't know for sure, but I do know that I've made a few mistakes about people in the past, so I have every reason to believe I was wrong about him too.

I go downstairs, make sure all the doors are locked, put the cat box with the new kittens in the broom closet for safety, empty the trash, and call my mother to tell her good night.